MAGEPUNK

Art of the Genre represents a huge shared world called *The Nameless Realms*, a place that spans thirteen extraordinary Ages of Man. Each category of fiction in this fantastic world has its own specialized medallion that is 'active' in the upper right corner of each book, thus allowing you to easily tell what specific genre you're purchasing. In the case of *Airship of Fools*, you're about to enter an age of Magepunk, set in the Eleventh Age of Man, so the medallion you see above is the symbol for all books in that field.

AIRSHIP OF FOOLS

SCOTT TAYLOR

Illustrated by
DAVID DEITRICK

Printed and bound in the United States of America 9 8 7 6 5 4 3 2 1

First edition: August 2014

ISBN: 978-1-940528-20-5

This is a work of fiction. All characters, places and events portrayed in this publication are either fictitious or used fictitiously.

Cover and Interior Illustrations: David Deitrick
Copy Editor Extreme: **Art of the Genre** Team
Graphic Design: Jeff Laubenstein
Book Design: John Woolley
Sounding Board: John O'Neill

Art of the Genre
217 Palos Verdes Blvd,
Redondo Beach, CA 90277

artofthegenre.myshopify.com

Ordering Information:
For details, contact the publisher at the address above.

*I'd like to dedicate this book to Noah McBrayer Jones for putting another character in my mind that kind of forced me to write a second novel in this series. Both he, and the lovely Kato from **Steampunk Couture**, helped me build another adventure in the setting of **The Gun Kingdoms**.*

*And as always, I'd like to put in one last thank you to all the fans on **Kickstarter** who made this dream a reality with their generous donations, and to artist David Deitrick who helped introduce me to steampunk with his incredible drawings for **Space: 1889**.*

CONTENTS

FOREWORD

Airship of Fools was a struggle, not only for the characters in the tale, but also for all the folks who were involved in it. Sometimes life just gets in the way of creation, and I believe that is what happened as David and I set out to make this book a reality.

Honestly, I'm not sure David thought he had it in him, but I kept at him over the course of a year until *Airship* was a reality.

In the end, I hope it is an enjoyable read and lends itself to the same type of adventure fantasy that the first one had. *The Gun Kingdoms* setting is an incredibly rich one to write in, and as I did research on the sky ships of our own world I was astounded by what adventures could be had in them. *Airship* grew from a painting called 'The Consultant' into what you now hold, and I hope I'll get a chance to visit this setting again before all is said and done because I think the characters have more stories to tell, but I guess we will all have to wait and see if that happens.

Thank you all again for your generous contributions in making this a reality and I truly hope that *Airship of Fools* was worth the wait.

Scott Taylor
May 29th 2014
Art of the Genre

ACKNOWLEDGEMENTS

With heartfelt thanks to all our Kickstarter backers!

Adventurer's Pass: Jeffrey Barnes, Kyle Pinches, Eric Puster, www.gnut.co.uk, Natalya Alyssa Faden, Mikael Olofsson

Captain's Cabin: Mark Wilkinson, **Shadow**, Gary Phillips, Andrew Findlay, Rhel

Airship Ace: Brett Bozeman, Charles Rutledge

GYPSY SKY (INTERIOR)

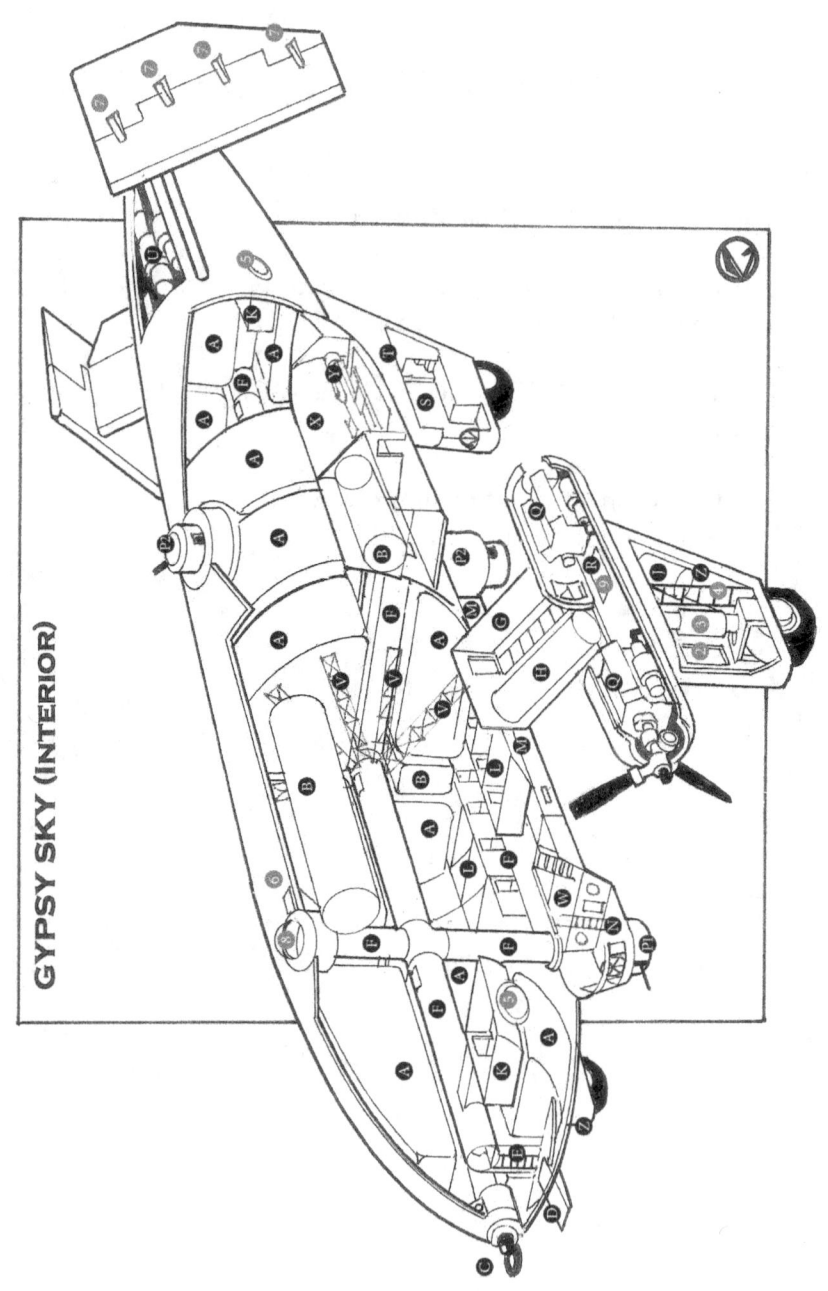

THE GYPSY SKY

A: Ballonets containing lifting gas
B: Hidden ballonets containing contraband organic lifting gas
C: Docking grapple for use when docking at a mast
D: Docking ramp with (docking) vestibule
E: Ladder from docking vestibule to "corridor"
F: The central corridor is called "Main Street"
G: Pylon connecting engine cars/landing gear
H: Fuel for engines
J: Lubricating oil for engines and landing gear
K: Adepts cabins (four cabins total P/S and F/A
 L: Cabins (singles for snobs, multiple bunks for crew)
M: Cargo holds
N: Main control room
P1: 1PDR quick-firing gun mounts
P2: 4 PDR recoiless gun mounts (ship-killers)
Q: Ship engines (4)
R. Hatch from engine room to landing gear spats
S: Tail wheel and auxiliary (ground-handling) control room
T: Stairs from aux. control room to stern of main body
U: Concealed emergency rocket boost engines: can be easily disconnected
    and discarded through kick-outs
V: Rigging – provides structural strength as well as access for teams
    inspecting ballonets
W: Captains day cabin
X: Gunboat storage bay
Y: Aerial gunboat.
Z: Landing gear spat
2: Door/hatch providing exit from landing gear spat – manned during
    take-off & landing
3: Shock absorber
4. Ladder to engine pod from LG spat
5. Observation lens-window for adepts
6. Topside access
7: Mass balance for control surfaces
8: Navigation astrodome for use with sextant
9: Optional swivel for 1PDR QF gun.

CHAPTER ONE

SKYLLA

Sometimes life gives you everything you've ever wanted, but the more I feel secure, the more I have to wonder when the bottom will fall out. You know this don't you, that all lives lived from the dawn of time are based on a series of ups and downs?

Still, I must stand in the light as long as I can. The ship is ours, the seas are ours, and as long as we remain at the crest of the wave, we should keep the course and try to sustain a lead that no darkness can catch...

Skylla moved up the deck, the calls of fishmongers and longshoremen filling the autumn air as dark birds fought for castoff scraps against gangs of smaller gulls. Tormay was at the plank, multi-buckled boots resting on the rail and a carbine in his lap.

He looked up from under his broad hat as she approached, two fingers sticking up to wave at her.

"Some guard you've turned out to be," she said.

Smiling, he looked up and down the deck, saying, "I see no brigands aboard, so I must be doing something right."

"Where's the captain?" she asked.

"Why, you looking for some kind of afternoon dalliance?"

She kicked his boots, and his legs fell to the deck as his hat slid off his head.

"Hey!" he said.

"You're lucky that's all you got and that I'm in a particularly good mood this morning. Now where is the captain?"

"He went ashore at dawn with Ugarth, I'd figure about a new cargo," Tormay said.

She frowned, looking back at the dock only to have her vision obscured by a flowered parasol.

"What the. . .?" she asked.

The white umbrella, delicate lace frills pinioned around its circumference, turned away and revealed a young lady with a mass of stark white hair pinned and styled atop her head. She wore a fine lavender dress, bodice cinched to expose as much of her pale breasts as civil decorum allowed.

Behind her a man stood, tall and broad in a deep grey suit and overcoat, his face a death-mask behind a trimmed white beard and smoothly shaven head.

"I'm sorry," the woman began. "I failed to see you there as I was taking in the ship's interesting lines."

Skylla took a step back, her hand slipping to one of the three knife sheaths at her hip. As her fingers grazed the hilt of a dagger stowed there, the man in grey burrowed a hand into his jacket and Tormay clicked the safety off his carbine.

"This is a private ship," Skylla said.

The woman smiled, the act both charming and venomous on her beautiful face. "Don't I know it..." she replied.

"I don't think you understand," Skylla began.

The woman held up a lace-gloved hand, "No, I'm afraid it's you that doesn't understand... Miss?"

"Skylla."

"Miss Skylla, this is my ship."

Skylla shook her head, "What?"

The smile remained as the woman drew down her parasol and clicked the stow-catch, answering, "Well, technically it's my husband's ship, but under Dragmarsh law what is Kaleb's property is mine and vice versa."

Skylla stood, mouth agape, as the woman pushed past her.

"Now, if you could show me to my husband's cabin, I'll settle in," the woman said.

Behind her the man in grey pulled his hand from his coat and picked up several pieces of luggage, his highly polished shoes making no sound as he moved up the plank.

"This can't be happening!" Skylla raged.

Mya, the ships Gola, pulled the circular, silvered cage from a glass, tea dripping from the thin cuts in its surface, and then reached for a jar of white honey.

"You do understand that you're still technically a slave?" the Gola asked.

Skylla turned, the bands at her wrists and neck burning as the element inside her raged to come to the surface.

"Of course I know that, but…"

"But what?" Mya interrupted, "We are both kept women, and as the captain is half a dozen years our senior and of noble blood, then he must have had a life to himself long before you or I were ever brought to this ship.

Skylla stared at the woman as the corner of her mouth twitched. Mya turned with a cup of tea in her hand, any seriousness in the conversation hidden by the folds of the translucent azure veil she wore over her face.

"In all the time you've spent with the captain, have you ever bothered to ask him if he was married?" Mya asked.

Taking the offered tea, Skylla shook her head, "No, but he wears no ring, and I assumed…"

"Assumptions are never a good thing, and as women, we must understand that men with his upbringing are likely to have been put into a political arrangement by their family at an early age," Mya interrupted again.

The tea was half to Skylla's lips when she pulled it back, "What does that mean?"

"It means, perhaps the captain doesn't wear a ring to signify the marriage because the marriage was never his idea in the first place. Certainly, in the eyes of the families involved and those of Dragmarsh, the man is married, but legality is rarely the true measure of a person's heart," Mya answered.

"Do you really believe that?"

Mya shrugged, "I'm very close to the captain as well, and he's never mentioned a wife to me, so I can only assume she isn't something he's fond of, and, atop that, probably a very good reason he enjoys being at sea rather than land."

"Because he can avoid situations like this…" Skylla whispered.

"Indeed."

"Well, if that's the case, what do I do?" Skylla asked.

"Give the captain space, as I'm sure he's even less pleased than you are to see her show up."

As if on cue, the sound of the Captain's raised voice echoed through the ship. Mya tilted her head, the slightest note of a smile showing through the veil.

"Thanks," Skylla said, getting to her feet.

"And remember, space means not going right…" but the Gola's words were lost in the clanking of Skylla's boots on the metal stair as she moved toward the captain's cabin.

Tolbert, Gates, and Greylin were lurking near the door to the captain's cabin as Skylla entered, all three scrambling and bumping into each other when she cleared her throat.

"Sorry ma'am," Gates said as he slipped past her.

Tolbert and Greylin made for the front of the vessel, their bare feet making no sound on the wooden planks as another round of the captain's shouts rang down the hall. Taking in a deep breath, Skylla moved forward until the word SkyGlaive was clearly uttered amid the up and down volume of the argument. It had clearly come from Kaleb, and Skylla slipped even closer, her hand resting on the polished wood of the doorframe.

Why would he tell her anything about our discovery of the map to that ship . . .

"An interesting conversation, no?"

The voice was thick, like sorghum spooned from a canning jar. Skylla turned, one of her throwing knives coming to her palm with practiced ease when the flare of a match illuminated the dark-bespectacled face of Kaleb's wife's porter. He was standing inside the arch of the ship's only passenger cabin.

"It's unwise to lurk in dark places on this ship," she replied.

The porter sucked hard on the end of a thin cigar, the orange glow making his eyes burn behind the lenses with an obsidian shine.

"Is it better to be lurking at closed doors then?" he asked.

She frowned, her armbands burning and the smell of the ocean filling the corridor. He raised a white eyebrow as the wave of elemental energy passed over him, but she took a steadying breath and sheathed her knife.

"I'd heard that the Sand Tyger had an Enlightened on board, but I wasn't inclined to believe it," he continued.

"Half-Enlightened," she corrected.

He drew another long inhale from the cigar, then, "I stand corrected, as I'm sure a full Enlightened wouldn't have even made it to the slavers' block; instead a public hanging would have been in order."

"I wonder how many would have died while trying to watch that," she said.

He drew the cigar from his mouth and pointed it at her neck and wrists, "Well, if those were in place, I'm sure it would have been safe enough."

Unconsciously, she rubbed the bands, the electric sting of them on her fingers making the hairs on the back of her neck stand at attention. Behind her, the volume of the argument rose again, and she turned back to the door.

"I'm sure this could go on for a while, so might I offer you a drink?" the stranger said.

She looked back, saying, "You're awfully bold for a servant."

He smiled, "Who said I was a servant?" Moving the cigar to his left hand, he offered her his right. Reluctantly she took it, and was pleased when his eyes widened at the feel of the power in her palm.

"The name is Noah McBrayer, and I'm the owner of CBH imports and exports, connoisseurs in the acquisition of the exotic."

So that's why you're here. Perhaps the loose lips on this ship let the existence of the SkyGlaive map slip, and it pulled you away from counting your blood-soaked coins...

"Nice to meet you," she replied.

They eyed each other a long moment, and she cursed him a dozen silent ways before releasing his hand.

"And what about that drink?" he asked.

She took one last sideways look at the captain's door, then nodded and followed him into his room. It wasn't much, and was rarely put to use as passengers weren't the usual cargo of the *Tyger*, but Noah had already unloaded half a steamer trunk that spilled all manner of strange trinkets over the bed and dresser in the room.

"I'm sorry there is only one bed, but the youngest members of the crew assure me that the deck is comfortable with the right bedding," she said.

Noah chuffed a laugh, "Ah, well, I'll have to take their word for it as Ms. Mallet has informed me she'll be staying in her husband's room, so this bed seems to be mine."

Bile rose in her throat, but she swallowed it down and managed a smile as Noah poured two shot glasses to the rim from an amber bottle stowed in a net on the steamer's interior lid. She took it, hammered it back, and then returned it before Noah could even begin his toast. He laughed again, poured her another, and this time offered his words of wisdom while the alcohol still filled the glass.

"May our journey together be a profitable one," he said.

She gulped the drink, and smiled back, "And exactly what do you know of this journey?"

"Only what Ms. Mallett tells me, which is that her husband, Captain Cross, has uncovered something that might lead to the final resting place of her father's fabled *SkyGlaive* Dreadnaught."

Skylla remembered when she'd found the map, deep beneath the Halo, and the shared memory that pressed itself into her mind when she'd first made contact with it.

The woman in the memory, could it have been some relation to Kaleb's wife? The hair, and the face, they did bear a striking resemblance...

"Is something wrong?" Noah asked.

She shook her head, the memories she'd had during the recovery of the map fading away as she came back to reality.

"No... must have been the drink. What is it anyway?" she asked.

Noah turned the bottle so she could see the label, a half-naked woman with flames for hair smiling back at her.

"Dravarian Fire Rum," he said.

"I thought the brewing techniques for making that were lost in the wars?" she asked.

Pouring her another glass, Noah shook his head, "If you, Miss Skylla, still exist, then who am I to question the possibility that Eldaryn brewers continue to lurk in places not yet found by bounty hunters and rogue mercenaries?"

She thought of Ethran Tha and her skin prickled.

My people are still out there, barely staving off extinction, and here I sit drinking their goods with a man who would exploit them even as they die…

She put the newly-filled glass down, and Noah watched her from beneath his dark spectacles.

"What makes you think Kaleb will take on a mission to find this fabled dreadnaught?" she asked.

"Kaleb is it? I'd have guessed you'd refer to him as Captain Cross, but perhaps this ship is more lax in titles than I anticipated. Whatever the case, Ms. Malett can be very persuasive. Truly, a woman of such beauty wouldn't have to work too hard to get into a man's good graces, or even his bed, now would she?"

Skylla's cheeks burned, and she wasn't sure if it was the drink or the slip of her tongue, but she stood and provided a hard-lipped smile.

"You don't give the captain enough credit," she replied.

As she turned to go, he called after her when she was in the doorframe, "Care to make a wager?"

She didn't reply, but slipped out into the hall where the heated exchange cooled off and the quiet made her skin crawl. Taking the forward stair to the deck, she moved to the rail as the Blood Moon hung high, and the Ghost was but a sliver at the edge of the sheltered harbor. Slipping out of her jacket and boots, she leapt the rail in a single motion and plunged into the water fifteen feet below.

There, beneath the surface, her heart calmed and she found a place to draw focus as the darkness around her soothed the fire in her blood.

CHAPTER TWO

KALEB

I'm not sure why this kind of luck follows me, maybe because I refuse to venerate Saint Erik, or perhaps because I built up too much bad karma in my military days, but whatever the case, I can't help feeling that I'm always waiting for the other shoe to drop.

Now, after more than four years, Vivian shows up with an ultimatum, and here I sit wondering if it is almost worth it to just walk away and let her have the Tyger. Then, I catch a whiff of reason and know that I can't do that to my crew, but worse yet, I know she knows that as well.

Whatever the future holds, there will be an ironclad contract in place after this mess is done to be sure it never, ever, happens again.

Kaleb watched his wife sleeping as he sat in his desk chair, hat before him and a quilted blanket over his torso. The room's single porthole provided crimson light from the Blood Moon and it turned Vivian's white hair pink, something that reminded him of spun-silk candy clouds he'd purchased at carnivals when he was young.

"You know you can join me," she whispered.

The words were barely audible, and she didn't move as she said them, so for a moment he sat perfectly still as though he'd imagined the offer.

Finally, she rolled over, her face porcelain, her large eyes oddly alien from the shading of coal she used. She was beautiful, but harsh, unless she smiled, in which case you felt the whispers of a thousand heady promises of love in your ears.

"You know we've shared a bed before, right?" she asked.

He nodded, but didn't reply.

"I didn't want this any more than you did, Kaleb, but sometimes to be gifted with noble blood in this life you must adhere to the costs of your station."

"I paid the dues of my station in the service of the military, and I'm not sure why this secondary contract was necessary," he replied.

She sat up on one thin arm, her hair, decorated in tattered silk ties that created two pigtails, fell down around her shoulders.

"I always knew I was secondary, but I didn't realize your children would be even further down the list," she said.

He sighed, his hands clenching beneath the blanket. "You took the children, Viv, as you knew I wouldn't dare follow you to the social centers of this broken world, and you wouldn't hear of me keeping them with me."

She laughed, "Keeping them? Here? The boys were 4 and 3, and your daughter a newborn and you wanted to bring them on this floating circus of danger?"

He shook his head, "That isn't fair. I didn't have to play the role I do..."

She cut him off, "Oh no, don't go making revisionist history concerning how you could have been an 'honest' trader living a calm life among sun-kissed archipelago seas. That isn't you Kaleb, and you can't deceive me and never could. You are a damnable crusader, a man for *all* people, and that is the reason you couldn't stay out of trouble or be with the true noble leadership of this world's nations."

"Noble leadership! Now you are trying to deceive me!"

"So we both have very different views of the world. I'd like to see my children raised by industrial moguls and political visionaries, and you'd like them suckled at the breast of a ship's Gola, or, worse yet, a half-Enlightened whore."

Kaleb was up before he realized it, blanket cast aside and one step away from the bed. Vivian, for all her venom, held her ground, her eyes dark and daring in the crimson light.

"Would you strike me?" she hissed.

With a growl, he turned and grabbed his hat and coat as he marched to the door.

"We will leave on the morrow for Mahe, or I'll have the ship impounded by the court!" she yelled after him.

He slammed the door, the smell of cigar smoke and alcohol thick in the hall outside. The door to the passenger suite clicked closed, and he turned to it, staring at the dark wood a moment before finally shrugging on his coat and making his way aft toward the bridge.

Slipping past the Gola's quarters, he made it to the command station and gave a great sigh when he saw Brandon Pascal seated in the captain's chair, a smile on his dark-skinned face.

"I thought I'd wait it out here," Brandon said.

Kaleb shook his head and moved to the navigator's station before throwing himself into a seat.

"She drives me crazy," Kaleb said.

"She always has, my friend," Brandon replied.

Kaleb took off his hat and ran his fingers through his long dark hair, "I just don't know how she could have found out so fast."

"This ship has too many tongues, but you already know that after the whole Elemental Core affair," Brandon said.

Kaleb sighed, "True, but I really didn't think Viv would be watching me this close. I mean, what we do really shouldn't be on her charts, unless something happened to disrupt her well-planned future."

"Maybe it has something to do with McBrayer," Brandon said.

"I guess it's possible. I've heard of him, and he's not really a man who runs in her circles, but that doesn't mean it wasn't her that brought him in on this and not the other way around."

Brandon nodded. "Whatever the case, he can't be trusted, not with some of the things I've heard about him."

"Noted, and by the Nine Isles of Hell, I'd throw him off this boat right now if I knew she'd let it go, but Viv never lets anything go," Kaleb added.

"So what's the plan?" Brandon asked.

"We go to Mahe, hire an airship from the Drifter Guild, and head east over the Madras."

Brandon sat up, "The Madras? Captain, there is a good reason no good Samaya would go onto or above the cursed sea. It is at the very heart of some of the last renegade strongholds of the Enlightened."

"That may be, but that is where the map indicates the SkyGlaive was kept, probably so it could deal death to the last of those bastions."

"Still, no one goes there, Kaleb, not unless they don't want to return. It is a graveyard for lost ships, both air and land."

Kaleb nodded, "Well, then it's a good thing you'll be staying with the Sand Tyger."

"Captain?"

"You heard me, I'm going with Viv and McBrayer, and if I don't come back, you and Skylla can decide what happens to the ship."

"Over my dead body," a voice added from the port stair.

Both men turned. Skylla, her skin still touched with a green hue, stood with hair dripping wet and her white pants and shirt nearly translucent.

"Skylla, I don't want any argument as I've had my fill tonight," Kaleb said.

"Then you just need to drop any thought of going into the Madras without me, and we don't have to argue at all," she replied.

Brandon got to his feet, but Kaleb motioned him to stay. "This concerns the whole crew, not just Skylla. I want both of you to call a meeting at sunrise, right after breakfast, so that at least everyone is good and well-fed before they hear this news. Otherwise, I'm going to get what sleep I can in the ready room."

He got up and moved to the door at the back of the bridge, but Skylla made it there before him.

"Captain," she said, eyes intense.

He sighed, nodded, and allowed her to enter. Before he followed, he looked back over his shoulder to Brandon. "Get the crew fed."

Brandon gave a quick salute, and then Kaleb closed the door.

Skylla pressed the map on the table, moving a few heavy rifle rounds to each corner to keep it down. Kaleb sat in a well-worn chair, his eyes drooping and his shoulders slumped.

"Do we really have to do this now?" he asked.

Skylla regarded him without expression, the skin on her arms covered in gooseflesh from the early morning chill and her plunge into the depths.

"If we don't get this settled now, we can't present a unified front for the crew," she said.

"A unified front would be me telling all of them that they aren't going, including you," he replied.

"Which is exactly the wrong decision since I'd have to countermand you in front of everyone."

He shook his head, "If you knew my wife, you'd understand what a bad decision this is,"

Skylla's cheeks flushed, and the smell of the ocean permeated the room. He leaned up, popped his neck, and then stared right into her green eyes. "Skylla, I've lived a strange life, and certainly the length of it was substantial before I ever came into ownership of the Tyger. I didn't speak about Viv... my wife, because for all intents and purpose we weren't married, at least not in any way that matters."

When she didn't reply, he continued. "We were married young, arranged by our families, and as much as I knew it wouldn't take, we did what we thought was right until we were finally forced to make the decision that living apart was much preferable to living together.

"I mean, I haven't worn my ring in years, not since she took the children and..."

"Children?" Skylla interrupted.

Kaleb sighed, "Yes, we have three, two boys and a girl."

Skylla turned away, her hands coming up to rub the cold out of her arms. Kaleb stood, drew off his coat, and tried to place it on her shoulders but she shrugged the attempt away.

"I don't need your pity, Captain, I'm a slave after all," she said.

He tossed the coat onto the table before reaching out and turning her around. She fought a moment until she looked into his eyes.

"I know this is raw and hard to understand, but don't let some piece of paper collecting dust in the files of Bureau of Licensing make you believe you are anything less than the woman I love," he said.

Her lips pressed tight, and he could see the conflict in them.

"And if you call yourself a slave again, I'll throw you off this boat myself, because we both know the truth of that," he continued.

She nodded, and he drew her close, their lips almost touching before a knock sounded on the door. They both jumped and stepped away from each other before Kaleb cleared his throat.

"Come," he said.

The door opened and the white-bearded face of Doc Rose leaned inside. He looked between them, adjusted his square-rimmed glasses, and asked, "Am I disturbing something?"

"No," Skylla said, with a bit too much verve.

Kaleb went back to his chair, "Come in, Doc."

"I'd spent the day in town, looking for some supplies, and hadn't heard about...," he paused, looked at Skylla, and then continued, "Vivian, until Brandon roused me."

"Yeah, she pretty much caught us all off guard," Kaleb said.

"Some more than others, I'm sure," Doc added.

Skylla moved around the table, her eyes on the map. "The captain says he's going to take an airship from Mahe into the Madras, and he's going to do it alone, no less."

Doc Rose raised an eyebrow and then adjusted his glasses, "You don't say?"

Kaleb shook his head, "You'd think a Captain could make decisions concerning his own person without being countermanded by his entire crew."

"Well, that is assuming his crew doesn't care about his well-being, or are smart enough to know when he's making pig-headed decisions," Doc replied.

"Exactly," Skylla added.

"So what would you have me do: ask for volunteers to go into the point of no return, or do you have everything already figured out?" Kaleb asked.

Skylla and Rose exchanged a look, and then turned to Kaleb as he rolled his eyes.

"Skylla, Stoneham, and I, will go with you, and one youngster for balance. I'd say Greylin," Doc Rose suggested.

"And you'll need someone with Mage-Tech, so I'd suggest Tolbert," Skylla offered.

"You two will be the death of me," Kaleb said.

"Quite the opposite, actually, but nonetheless, you should be sure to tell the crew your strategy when you meet with them in an hour," Rose said.

Kaleb watched them a moment before finally throwing his hand in the air, 'Fine! But can I get some sleep at the very least?"

Doc Rose smiled and moved back to the door, Skylla following him. "Why don't we get you some hot tea, girl. Otherwise you might be too sick to travel," the doctor suggested.

Skylla helped him through the door before looking back at Kaleb. He nodded, and a brief smile fought its way onto her lips before losing the battle. Then she was gone.

Banished Gods, why does it have to be this way? They shouldn't risk themselves for a problem of my making, but there's no talking them out of it, and the truth is that I'll need them out there…

Leaning back in his chair, he closed his eyes and let the darkness come, sleep taking him before he could fully compose his thoughts into a speech for the meeting.

The crew was on deck, seabirds playing in the rigging of the tall ships. Among the sailing vessels steamers leaked black smoke. A deep and soaking morning mist hung over the bay. Kaleb stood with his coat drawn up around his chin, a drop of condensation hanging from the brim of his hat.

Around him, on coils of rope, crates, and barrels, the crew of the Sand Tyger sat, each with an expression that mirrored his own: placid.

"By now I'm sure you've heard the rumor that my wife is on board and that she's looking to mount a venture into the Madras," he began.

Murmurs rose at the mention of the cursed inland sea.

"That much is true, but this ship won't be going there, only a handful of others and I will be making that journey."

More murmurs, but they were quieted when Stoneham raised his voice with a scathing, "Stow it, you lot!"

"We'll be taking the Tyger to Mahe, and from there I'll hire an airship to take us across the middling ranges to the east. I'm going to give it a month, and if we can't find what we're looking for, will head back. But if, for some reason, we don't return, Mr. Pascal will take command of the Tyger and you'll treat him as your new captain."

Silence this time, and he took a minute to walk back and forth as the words sunk in.

"Who is coming with you, captain?" Ensign Tucker Parish asked.

Kaleb turned to regard the kid, only just turned sixteen and already more competent with the ship's functions than most of the crew.

" Skylla, Stoneham, the Doc, Greylin, and I," he answered.

Parish rose to his feet, "But, captain, I've more experience than Grey..."

"That's enough, Mister Parish," Stoneham cut him off.

Parish pursed his lips and clenched his fists, but finally heaved a sigh before retaking his seat.

Kaleb looked at Doc Rose, who regarded him with the edge of a smile beneath his white beard, and then at Skylla. She eyed him, seemingly read his mind, and then walked over to whisper nonsense in his ear before stepping away with arms crossed behind her back.

"It seems my first mate will need a porter for the trip, if there is anyone who..."

"I volunteer, captain!" Parish said, leaping to his feet.

Kaleb nodded and then regarded the rest of the small crew, good men and women all.

"Let's get this boat ready to sail, as the sooner we can make Mahe, the sooner we can get this over with," he instructed.

Men got up and moved to their respective positions, Parish coming forward to give him a crisp salute before he ran off toward the bridge.

"That was a good thing you did," Doc Rose said.

The older man now stood beside him wiping mist from his glasses with a handkerchief.

"When I have to bury the boy, I'll remind you of those words," Kaleb replied.

Rose shook his head, "Don't go burying any of us just yet. We've survived worse than rumors of cursed seas and old maps."

From the far side of the pontoon Kaleb saw a match flare and a dark figure slip inside the hatch to below decks.

"I assure you, it's not rumors or maps that worry me..."

CHAPTER THREE

SKYLLA

There was a time when I thought our Gola was my enemy, a time when I was convinced it was she who wanted the man I loved, but now I've come to find a viper lurks in the veneer of a marriage vow: one who walks the ship as though she owns it.

I don't care what the common laws of Findalynn say. If I had my choice, I'd deliver her quickly to the sea and be done with it, but I know Kaleb would never allow such a thing. Still, I can't get over what she represents, or worse yet, what the children she has delivered mean to Kaleb. They are the tie that binds, no matter what I'd like to do to the mother, and no matter what steps I take with Kaleb in the future. That, is something I'm not sure I can stand.

The ocean was clear as the *Sand Tyger* fought against the trades coming up from the Isles of Autumn toward Mahe Bay. Skylla stood at the rail of the starboard pontoon, her eyes watching the leaping play of a pod of Castro's Dolphins. The creatures were green as emeralds with a single blue stripe down their sides that made them almost invisible in their native kelp forests that dotted the southern coast. At times like this they would come to race the faster ships of the Halo.

"They're beautiful," a woman's voice said.

Skylla turned, Vivian Mallet having moved up the deck to stand next to her. The woman wore an impressive amount of clothing, a chemise, underskirt, drawers, stockings, and corset were accessorized with short-heeled lace-up boots, gloves, and a parasol.

Looking back at the water, Skylla didn't reply. Ms. Mallet sighed, drew closer, and ran her gloved hand over the rail.

"How long have you been with him?" Vivian finally asked.

Skylla bristled, the palms of her hands growing wet and her heart thrumming in her ears.

"He's a tough one to resist," Mallet continued, "as the Banished Gods could attest from the actions of my youth."

"What do you want?" Skylla hissed.

Mallet didn't answer, but instead leaned out over the rail so that the sun caught her face and shown against the paleness of it.

Finally, Skylla turned to regard her, and Mallet pulled back beneath the parasol and smiled.

"I've heard you will travel with the party into the Madras," Mallet said.

"I go with the captain," Skylla replied.

"Yes, you would of course, but I'll have you know I'll protect my husband with my life," Mallet said.

Words of protest were halfway out of Skylla's mouth before she froze.

Mallet continued smiling, slowly spinning the parasol so the flowers printed on it cast a strange rainbow of color down on her face.

"Kaleb may no longer be mine, but that doesn't invalidate what he is, or what we once had, no matter what he, or you, might think," Mallet sighed.

Pushing away from the rail, she slid past Skylla, but before she was gone, she leaned close, whispering, "Remember, he is *my* husband."

Skylla stood a long moment, bile rising in her throat. Beneath the pontoon the dolphins continued to play, their chirps drifting up to her ears above the lap of the waves.

Her husband! Kaleb, what other secrets are you hiding beneath that unreadable façade?

Mahe was known as the City of Jade, the bronze rooftops having turned deep green over the millennia it had been in existence. It was one of the first cities rebuilt by the Enlightened when they came out of the Shining Cities as a gift to the suffering Samaya. In return, the swelling Samaya population was one of the first to join the alliance against the Enlightened before the great wars. No good deed ever goes unpunished.

Now the venerable city stretched out around its deep-water bay like a green serpent, and mighty towers rose skyward from the body where airships hung in the sky like gulls cruelly tethered to the back of a steamer by fishing line.

Skylla stood on the gangplank, Stoneham next to her and Parish coming up the pontoon with a hat pulled down around his brows and a satchel over one shoulder.

"You know we aren't leaving on a trip today, right?" Stoneham asked.

Parish gave a sheepish grin and nodded, "I know, but it's always better to be prepared."

Stoneham looked at Skylla and shook his head, "This one is best left on the bridge."

She was about to respond when the doors to the port deckhouse opened and Ms. Mallet walked onto the deck. Stoneham gave a whistle, and Tormay, standing on the port gun nacelle, nearly tumbled out of his station as he got a good look at her.

The woman was wearing an ermine dress touched with pale crimson accents, and her bodice squeezed her breasts up into twin snowy mounds beneath her pointed chin. Kaleb followed her, his wide-brimmed hat and weathered duster now replaced by hair oil and a fine black suit. Absently, he pulled with crooked finger at his white collar held with a black tie around his neck.

"She's beautiful..." Parish whispered.

Stoneham pulled the youth's hat down over his eyes and Parish cursed and swatted at the obscuring hand.

"Women like that are for noble-born, kid, so looking is about as close as you'll ever get."

Kaleb's dark hair was oiled back, and his mustache had been trimmed and waxed, the attire a perfect match to that of his wife. Skylla couldn't take her eyes off him, and her stomach churned with a mix of emotion.

Saint Shera, give me the strength to survive this...

McBrayer appeared next, his grey coat and burgundy vest beneath topped with a bowler that had a matching colored feather sprouting from a silk ribbon around the bowl.

"Looks like they'll be attending the Jade Magistrate's dinner tonight while we have the duty of securing a ship," Stoneham said.

Parish, finally free of his hat, pushed his disheveled hair from his eyes and added, "I've never seen the Captain look so uncomfortable."

Skylla shook herself from her torpor and nodded, "Right, we know our jobs, Stoneham, so no need to hang about the plank."

She started down the incline when Kaleb's voice brought her to a halt. She bit her lip, but turned and kept her composure as the well-dressed company made it to the pontoon's exit.

"You know the needs?" Kaleb asked.

Skylla nodded, "Yes Captain, we went over it a dozen times before we made port."

Mallet placed a hand on Kaleb's lapel and Skylla stiffened. "She understands, Kaleb, or why else would you have made her your first mate?"

Nodding, Kaleb once again pulled at his collar, saying, "Right, well, I just want to make sure…"

"We've got this, captain, now go and enjoy your night," Stoneham cut in.

Kaleb regarded the quartermaster, then Skylla, and finally nodded. His wife took his arm, and he made an uncomfortable pilgrimage down the plank and onto the docks, McBrayer following behind like a gloomy shadow.

"I don't trust that guy," Parish said.

"Me either, kid, but the Captain knows what he's doing, so let's just keep our noses to the business at hand, right Skylla?"

She didn't answer, instead watching the trio disappear further up the dock where it intersected with the first city street.

"Skylla?"

She turned, "Huh? Oh, yeah, let's get this trip of ours over so we can focus on more important things."

Stoneham started down the plank, Parish on his heels but Skylla grabbed the kid's shoulder and held him up.

"Ditch the pack," she said.

Parish nodded, sighed, and then tossed the pack back onto the pontoon.

"Where we're going the last thing we're going to need is something to weigh us down," she said.

The streets of Mahe were once an intricate latticework of planned thoroughfares, but as the Samaya took control of the city and poverty spread, the permanent and patina-covered buildings were cobbled onto by temporary dwellings. Now, the city seemed like a fungal covered skeleton that was being devoured by some insidious spore, and the people here added to the feeling.

Shadowed figures lurked among the tangle of buildings, some of which leaned precariously over the street, and on corners gangs of men huddled around smoking braziers, and children ran wild along the dank and oil-filled gutters.

"And I thought Findalynn had its problems," Parish whispered.

"Stow it, kid, we don't want anyone hearing your astute observations and taking offense," Stoneham said.

Above them a tower rose into the sky as light from the fading day painted the clouds in a cascade of pink and violet hues. Shadowed lines marked the base of the spire further up the block, a haphazard brick wall and some barbed wire keeping the local population from trying to scale it. At a single entrance, a large man with a double barrel scattergun puffed on a cigarette offered to him by a woman in the tattered and knee-muddied dress of a prostitute.

"Seems like a nice place," Stoneham offered.

"I bet the captain is having a better time of it," Parish added.

"Keep quiet, both of you," Skylla hissed. "We need to act the part of interested parties with cash to spare, not sea sailors gawking and gossiping like schoolgirls."

Stoneham straightened up, and Parish adjusted his silly hat. Skylla pulled her violet hair back, tied it in a knot, and then wrapped it in a scarf she'd borrowed from Mya. Once done, she rolled down her sleeves and buttoned the collar of her jacket, the oricalcum slave bands disappearing from sight.

"Ok, Stoneham, you take the lead, but don't get too cute," Skylla said.

Stoneham nodded and the trio approached. The man with the gun spied them when they were twenty feet out and handed the cigarette back to the whore before adjusting his weapon to a two-hand grip.

"What can I do for ya?" he asked.

"We're lookin' for wings," Stoneham replied.

"I got wings, darlin', and I promise to make you fly," the whore offered.

The man threatened to strike her with the butt of his gun, and she slunk away, a greasy-tooth smile passing her lips as she gave Parish a final wink.

"Sorry bout that. Old Grace doesn't know nothin' about acting around respectable folk," the man said.

"Not like I haven't seen her type before, but nonetheless, we'd be needin' to see the captains," Stoneham replied, mimicking slightly vocal inflections of the man.

The guard scratched the grey-speckled stubble at his chin and nodded.

"Yeah, well, they're busy folk, the captains," he said.

Stoneham reached into his coat and the man raised his weapon. The quartermaster froze a moment, then showed his hand. A leather-strap wallet with the corners of some gold-notes hanging out changed the man's expression.

"Right, well let me think a moment about how busy they are," the man said.

Stoneham nodded, drew out two twenty-buck notes and offered them up. They disappeared in a flash, and the man quickly slung his weapon.

"Still, they might not be as engaged as I might have first thought," the man said.

Taking a step back, he moved to an iron door in the wall and jingled a set of keys. Above the portal a bronze emblem was hung depicting an airship against the setting sun. Both the door and the sign had seen better days.

The creaking protest of rusted hinges echoed as the door swung inward and the man waved out his hand to invite them in. Skylla was the last to enter, and the surroundings inside the wall were no less begging for a fire than the streets beyond.

An open end of an elevator stood beneath the four steel pillars of the tower at the wall's center, a fine collection of rust having settled on all surfaces. Two men sat at a table before the shaft playing a game of cards, but neither paid attention to the newcomers until the guard spoke up.

"New clients for the captains," he said.

One of the men nodded, and the other chuffed a laugh. From the shadows a boy a handful of years younger than Parish appeared, adjusting a small hat with a polished leather strap under his dirty chin.

"Gram, see these people to the Tethered Barrel," the guard said.

"Yessir," Gram saluted.

The boy moved to the elevator, threw a lever, kicked the mechanism, and then smiled as a whirring sounded and chains began to rise and fall.

"Gram will take you up," the guard pointed to the sky.

There, bound by half a hundred ropes, three dark shapes hung suspended in air with thin bridges going from their superstructure to the tower at the center.

"Only three captains are in, but I'm sure you'll find what yer lookin' for," the guard smiled.

"Thanks," Stoneham said.

The guard moved off, and Stoneham slid close to Skylla, whispering, "Why did Kaleb pick this tower for us to check?"

She sighed, answering, "Because it was likely the only one with desperate enough captains to take on our fool's commission."

The elevator clanged to a halt, precariously shaking as Gram braced himself and then pushed the inner cage door open. Once the folding metal panel was out of the way, he slid the outer door from their path as music and smoke poured into the cage with equal vigor.

Gram bowed, and Stoneham slipped him a gold-note which he slipped under his cap.

"Is that a music box?" Parish asked.

"No, it's got to be a phonograph," Stoneham replied.

"Sounds kind of haunting all the same," Parish added.

The three of them stepped into the center of a tavern, circular in design and housing a dozen un-shuttered windows that allowed in a cool breeze and the din of airship coils spooling in the dusk.

A pall of blue-green smoke hung about the upper rafters, and two dozen men sat at tables or around a bar that curved from one side of the room toward the elevator. The music, a thrumming tune of war, came from a conical horn near the bar, and a man in old military dress slumbered next to it with an overturned tankard still clutched in a weathered hand.

The barkeep, a man of middling years and receding hairline, nodded as they entered, and Stoneham made for him, Skylla on his heels and Parish just behind.

She kept her head turning, each collection of men watching her as she went.

Three groups, and three captains, each one of them looking like the central spoke of a wheel...

"What brings you to the Tethered Barrel?" the barkeep asked as they drew close.

"Whiskey," Stoneham ordered.

"Two," Parish held up a duo of fingers.

The barkeep nodded, and Skylla slid onto a stool before swiveling around so her elbows rested on the bar and her eyes on the bulk of the curving room.

As the two shots were being poured, Stoneham started in, "We're looking for transport."

"Ya don't say?" the barkeep smiled.

"Yeah, do ya think you can steer us in the right direction?"

"Well, there are many a captain who uses the Barrel as his home port of call, but only three currently are in residence, and one of those has already taken on a contract."

Skylla let her eyes travel back and forth between the three larger gangs of men. At the center of the first was a man with smashed face and multiple earrings, his crew reflecting his unpleasant beauty, and he'd yet to take much notice of their presence.

This captain already has a cargo...

The second was a tall man with dead eyes, and he had as many knives about his leather belts as the first captain had earrings. The crew was no less armed, and they had a predatory nature about them, each one staring back at her without blinking.

Pirates, or at least opportunists...

"Where might you be headed, and that could help me make a recommendation," the barkeep continued.

"We're looking to set a course east," Stoneham replied.

The barkeep stopped rubbing his apron on the bar and cleared his throat.

"East?" he asked.

"Yep, and that's about all any captain would need know no," Stoneham answered.

Skylla found the third captain, a rotund man with ruddy cheeks and shock of white hair that made a ring around his bald pate. His crew was busy rolling dice, and the few that paid her attention were making unveiled reference to the size of her chest.

"We won't find a captain here tonight," she said.

Stoneham turned, and Parish croaked as he tried to drink his whiskey.

"What?" the barkeep asked.

"I said that no captain here will either take us on or has the necessary skills we are looking for," she replied.

Pushing off from the bar, she tapped Parish on the shoulder and he quickly placed his half-drunk shot on the bar as Stoneham paid the tab.

"You always let your woman make decisions for you?" a voice came from further down the bar.

Skylla turned, as did the others. A man no older than Kaleb seated alone at the bar's end slowly brought a glass to his mouth. He was thin for a man of his age, dressed in a green leather coat with goggles about his neck and a shock of white-blond hair tucked beneath a red cap on his head. A crimson scarf was tucked about his neck, gold runes sown delicately into the fabric.

"You stow yer talk, Charles. These are honest folk," the barkeep said.

Charles chuckled, took the rest of his drink in a single gulp, and then slammed the glass down on the bar.

"Honest folk don't come to the Barrel, nor do they look to travel East," Charles said.

"Let's go," Stoneham said.

Skylla nodded, but Charles stretched his back and turned, his eyes dark with ash beneath them, and his face handsome and angled with a thin layer of stubble. She paused, and he grinned at her.

"I said you keep yer yap shut," the barkeep broke in.

"What's the problem, Gavin. You'll take my money for drink but not let me solicit like other captains?" Charles asked.

The barkeep hissed a laugh, "Yer no captain, and that ship of yours won't fly. Of that I'm certain."

Stoneham leaned in, "You heard the man, let's be off and leave this mess for tomorrow. Perhaps more ships will be in by then."

No, tomorrow will make no difference once they hear where we're going...

She took a step down the bar, shaking her arm away from the grasping hand of Stoneham.

"So which is it, Mr. Charles. Do you have a ship or not?" she asked.

The man's smile broadened, "It's Rutledge. Charles's my first name. But to answer your question—yes, I've got a ship."

The barkeep bristled at this, hands flying wide, "Miss, please, this man is a charlatan. He's a former sailor, to be sure, but no ship will have him now after…"

As he trailed off, Skylla looked between the two men, the barkeep red-cheeked and Charles calm as an executioner.

"After what?" she asked.

"After my last ship was lost east of Newburrow," Charles replied.

She looked at Parish, who whispered, "Newburrow is the furthest city east of the Aflyr coast, and lies along the inlands."

"Do you have a crew?" she asked.

"I do if you're willing to hire me… say, one thousand gold-notes, and two thousand when we return from wherever you're headed?"

The barkeep scoffed. Conversations around the bar had quieted since the phonograph had dimmed them.

"Three thousand…" Stoneham hissed.

"It's a deal, Mr. Rutledge, assuming the ship will actually fly," she said.

"Skylla?" Stoneham broke in.

She turned and put a hand on his shoulder, whispering, "McBrayer is paying the tab, so I feel no remorse, and besides, what are the odds we'll actually return?"

A smile crossed the quartermaster's lips, and he nodded. "Good point."

"Then we have a deal," Rutledge said as he stood and offered his hand. She didn't take it, instead bowing and heading for the elevator. Over her shoulder, she asked, "And where can we find you and your ship?"

"Maxum and Templemount, Hanger Eight," Charles called after her.

"We'll see you there on the morrow, and I'd better be impressed," she replied.

Gram already had the door open, and, when she turned around, she saw Charles still smiling at her as the doors of the elevator closed.

CHAPTER FOUR

KALEB

I remember the days when I was forced to dress up and be presentable for the guests of my father. It was never something I enjoyed, and when I went into the military I enjoyed the starched collars and dress codes even less, but here I am in this fool suit like a Findalynn barrister.

I can only hope that Skylla understands this sacrifice and that she finds the transport we seek; otherwise I'm not sure this night could be any more miserable.

The plates were being cleared, and the men were gathering at the door of the study with brandy and cigars close at hand. Kaleb watched the ladies, all in lace and pinioned hair, moving toward the parlor, and he eyed the exit to the building's veranda.

Vivian caught his eye, the black pigments around hers drawn out toward her ears giving her the appearance of a predatory cat, but nonetheless she was by far the most lovely creature among the ladies.

She nodded toward the study, and he frowned.

You've been too long removed from me, my dear, as you've forgotten that the fastest way to make me not do what you'd like is to command it…

Turning from the gathering men, he grabbed a trundle-down candle and moved toward the veranda. A servant moved to intercept him, but one stern look and the man backed down until he entered the cool night air and breathed deep.

Banished Gods, these nights remind me why I fled to the sea...

"Nice night to take in the Ghost Moon, no?" a man's voice asked.

Kaleb turned to see Magistrate Bozeman's youngest son standing along the stone rail that led to the gardens below.

"Indeed," Kaleb said.

He placed the candle on the rail and reached into his coat for a cigar. The young man looked up at the silvery disc in the night sky, it's lower half already taking on the pink shading of its oncoming bloody sister.

"I'm surprised you aren't smoking with father and the rest of his esteemed company," the young man said.

Kaleb shrugged, bit the end off the cigar, and leaned down to the candle. After a few long puffs, he sighed and closed his eyes.

"That hard huh?" the young man continued.

"Indeed," Kaleb said again.

Footsteps drew closer and he opened his eyes and offered a hand.

"I'm Brett, as I don't think we were ever properly introduced," the young man said.

Kaleb shifted the cigar to his left hand and shook with his right, the young man's grip practiced and solid.

"Kaleb Cross," he offered.

"Yes, I know, and your wife is something of a story teller where you are concerned," Brett replied.

Kaleb took a drag, then, "Is she?"

The couples had been customarily broken up during the dinner, and he'd been stuck with an industrialist's second wife and the son of a prominent Mahe banker, but Vivian had been closer to the head of the table near the Magistrate and evidently his son.

"Yes, she said you own a ship that was something of a legend during the wars?"

"The Sand-Tyger, but I think my wife overstates the qualifications as the ship never saw any action during that conflict."

Brett nodded, "Well, I'm sure it's still something to see. I've only read about some of the ships used during that time, but I hope to one day see one."

"I'd stick to dinner parties and counting money, certainly a much safer pursuit," Kaleb said.

"Not for me, I've gone to university in Tiefon, and I want to become an archeologist, maybe try to figure out why the Enlightened turned on us," Brett offered.

Kaleb raised his eyebrow, "Is that what they teach you at university, that the Enlightened turned on the Samaya?"

Brett nodded, "Yes… I mean, there are those that theorize it was a more mutual affair, but that kind of discussion is frowned upon."

"I'd suppose it is…"

"Do you have another opinion Mr. Cross?"

"I do, and call me Kaleb."

Brett smiled, "Can I hear it, Kaleb?"

After another long puff on the cigar, he looked up at the moon, saying, "The Samaya feared what the Enlightened could do, and once they realized they could make their own rules, they decided it was best for everyone if the Enlightened were eliminated, thus leveling the playing field for all that remained."

Brett didn't reply, and finally Kaleb turned to look at the young man. He stood ashen faced, his close-cropped blond hair, spectacles, and thin frame marking him more for books than an honest day's work.

"Does that shock you?" Kaleb asked.

Brett shook his head, "No… I mean, I'd heard stuff, but, well… no."

"Then that is your first step, Mr. Bozeman, and if you heed it, then you might make a fine archeologist."

Looking up, Brett provided a slight smile before asking, "Mr. Cross… er, Kaleb, if you don't mind me asking, Mrs. Mallet, she said you were going on a trip to the East."

Kaleb nodded.

"If you need someone with a certain knowledge base, I'd be happy to offer my services."

"And what would your father say to that?" Kaleb asked.

"My father doesn't much care what I do, Sir, as I've got three older brothers and two sisters. I'm assuming it wouldn't be too draining on his bank accounts."

Kaleb laughed and took another puff on his cigar.

"Well, I can't offer you the promise of a safe return, but I've never been one to deny a man's desire to prove himself, especially if he's willing to see the truth."

"Do you mean it, sir?"

"Mr. Bozeman, if your father allows it, then I'm glad to have you."

Brett laughed, stifled it, and then excused himself. Kaleb smiled as he looked back up at the Ghost Moon.

What tricks are you playing at now, old moon?

Taking another long draw on the cigar, he shook his head and closed his eyes once more, the smell of the sea heavy on the breeze.

"Mr. McBrayer secured the travel papers," Vivian said.

"I'm not surprised he did, as that was the reason for tonight, wasn't it?" Kaleb replied.

Vivian sighed, reached out and slid her arm under his, her head falling to his shoulder. Behind them McBrayer walked, his footfalls echoing on the cobbled streets as they moved down from the high district toward the docks.

"You know you could have helped him," she said.

"I'm sure he had it all under control and I'd have only complicated matters. Better to let the man do his business in peace."

"Why must you always be so withdrawn when it comes to society?" she asked.

"Why must you always be so accepting of those who live in it?"

She laughed, a tiny little sound that sent gooseflesh up his neck.

I hate it when her laughs are real, like that. There was a time when I enjoyed them, but that was before this veneer took over and the girl I grew up with turned into something else...

"You know, there was a moment tonight when I thought you might actually be enjoying yourself," she said.

"Oh?"

"Yes, when you were discussing the Halo current and its impact on trade costs."

He looked down at her, but only her white hair could be seen, piled and plated as is was on the top of her head.

"How could you possibly have heard that story?"

"You are my husband and we were in a formal setting. It is my duty to be able to hear as much as I can from the table, especially where you are concerned."

Kaleb shook his head, "I'll never understand why you put so much stock in such things."

"It is either that or fall into obscurity."

"Obscurity has its rewards," he replied.

She squeezed herself closer to his arm, asking, "And would you have been as happy with me in your obscurity?"

"It was a political marriage, Viv. How many times do we have to discuss it?"

"Until you admit the truth," she said.

He sighed, but didn't reply. After a minute she spoke again, this time with a wistful tone in her voice.

"Samuel reminds me of you."

"I wouldn't know," he replied, an edge of steel in his voice.

"You could know, but your stubborn streak won't allow it, just as your son refutes every word that escapes my lips."

"We've been round and…" he broke off.

Ahead, four dark shapes drifted from the shadows of one of the overhanging buildings. They were tall, lean, and at least one carried a long weapon. Kaleb pushed Vivian behind him, his hand instinctively going to his hip but his pistol wasn't there.

"Damn social propriety," he hissed.

"Now don't go getting ideas, mate, as ya can end this quick with a delivery of the lady or your wallet. 'Tis your choice," one of the figures offered.

The Blood Moon, having finally taken full control of the night sky, shown down on the men as they moved closer, each dirty, scruff-bearded, and carrying some type of improvised weapon.

"I've got this, Mr. Cross," McBrayer said as he walked past.

The man was removing his jacket as he went, handing it to Kaleb, and then beginning to roll his sleeves. Before he could get the second piece of fabric properly aligned on his forearm, one of the men leaped forward with a cry.

The thief swung a pipe overhand, but McBrayer sidestepped and brought one of his meaty fists into the man's face. Blood sprayed out as the man tumbled back with his nose spread half across his face.

There was a moment of stunned silence. Then the leader adjusted his grip on a cudgel and half shouted, "You'll pay for that!"

He came on but was more reserved, swinging the weapon horizontally to keep McBrayer from getting close. The other two tried to flank

McBrayer, but he slid back, both arms ready in fisticuff fashion, and Kaleb moved Vivian back as well while handing her McBrayer's coat.

"You better take this," he said.

As he made the exchange, Vivian slipped something warm and metallic into his hand. He looked down and caught the flash of scrollwork on a polished metal hold-out pistol, the twin barrels no more than two inches in length.

He glanced back at her and she gave him an innocent expression. He turned back to the combat just as McBrayer deflected a blow from the cudgel on his forearm and shouldered past the leader's defense.

Now behind him, another man raised a knife, but Kaleb adjusted his grip on the pistol and fired a single shot. The knife dropped as the man let out a scream and clutched his shoulder. McBrayer didn't flinch at the sound of the shot. Instead, he wrested the cudgel from the off-balance leader and beat him to the ground with three quick swings.

The fourth man made a quick retreat, his bare feet slapping on the cobbles as the groans and curses of the three others filled the night air.

McBrayer, now splattered with blood on his white shirt, cast the cudgel aside and turned back to Kaleb.

"My thanks," he said.

"You can thank Vivian, as it was her weapon," Kaleb offered.

McBrayer nodded, "All the same, I'll leave my thanks where they were."

He moved forward and took his coat from Vivian, then returned to the distance he'd been keeping before the walk was interrupted.

Kaleb blew out the barrel of the hold-out, flipped it over, and then handed it back to Vivian, saying, "I don't even want to know where you got that.

She smiled as she took it, but didn't reply, instead slipping in close once more so she could hold his arm as they walked.

"You know," he continued, "I taught you to shoot, so you could just have easily dealt with that man."

"And what kind of lady would I be if I did so?" she asked.

He let out a laugh, and she joined in with one of her own.

Banished Gods, there it is again. No, this is not going to be easy, not if she's going to play nice...

Kaleb stood on the deck of the ship with a small collection of duffels around him as well as the bulk of the crew. Greylin was next to Parish, the former four years older, a head taller, and handsome as a spring morning with his long dark hair and cobalt eyes.

Stoneham was with them, the quartermaster having his front-brim hat backwards and stroking one of his sideburns. Beside him stood Tolbert, roughly the same age as Greylin although thinner and with the rune-embroidered scarf of his trade wrapped around his neck.

Doc Rose and Skylla rounded out the party, the two of them waiting at the plank as Vivian came on deck with McBrayer hauling both their trunks, his the smaller that was tucked up under his chin.

"The man is strong. I'll give him that," Stoneham whispered.

"Indeed, but I'd wager Yogo could out-lift him," Kaleb replied.

Stoneham continued to stroke his sideburn, but gave no other reply. When the duo made it to where the rest stood, McBrayer continued on down the plank with his load, while Vivian pulled up with a smile. Nodding to her, Kaleb turned to Brandon and offered his hand.

They shook, Brandon saying, "I'll keep the ship in top shape for your return."

"I know you will, but if we…"

"You will, sir, I'm sure of it," Brandon finished.

Kaleb sighed and walked down the plank, Vivian and the rest of the crew following. Skylla stayed at a distance, and Kaleb went with Stoneham at his side while Greylin took up a position in the rear.

"You're sure this captain has a ship?" Kaleb asked for the fourth time.

"Skylla seemed to think so, and she's the first mate," Stoneham replied.

"Well, I sent her for a reason, I just don't like it that we aren't headed to an air dock but instead a ground hanger," Kaleb said.

"The barkeep didn't like that guy, and from the sound of things he'd already lost a ship someplace to the East, so not a sterling reputation to be sure," Stoneham said.

"I guess we'll wait and see, but I fear this man's ship isn't going to be what I'd hoped."

As if to punctuate the statement the morning bells began to toll, and the sun peeked through the marine layer in bright columns that fell on this city like beams from heaven.

The company walked down slick streets, and the workers in dark garb were out in force heading toward textile mills; children moved in packs toward schools, and women hung laundry on lines that spanned the streets above their heads.

When they made the junction of Maxum and Templemount, they found a collection of decrepit hangers, old surplus from the Final War and long abandoned to the forces of nature.

Hanger Eight was no less tumbledown than the rest, although no chains bound its twin doors. Kaleb came forward and knocked on the smaller personnel door set into the large sliding panels of the hanger proper. Rust fell from the spot he pounded, but the door held and after a moment a latch was thrown and the portal opened.

A man stood in the door, goggles over his eyes and a set of heavy leather gloves and apron adorning him.

"Ah, you're earlier than expected, but nonetheless, come in," he said.

Kaleb looked back at Skylla, her face implacable.

"What an interesting turn of events," Vivian said, the edge in her voice mocking.

Kaleb didn't reply, instead moving inside as his eyes adjusted to the gloom. A handful of still intact glass panels in the roof illuminated the interior with yellow light, and amid that glow a long cylindrical ship hung from chains attached to giant pylons running the length of the hanger.

"That's an old GX-23," Tolbert said.

"No, the 23 had six engines and a less conical front housing. That one's got neither," Stoneham said.

"It's been modified, but the frame and lift cells are from a 23 for sure," Tolbert continued.

"Will it fly?" Kaleb asked.

The man who opened the door, introducing himself as Captain Charles Rutledge, began cleaning his goggles with a dirty rag and added, "I can assure you it will fly, Mister?"

"Cross, and this is my crew," he waved to those gathered, then to Vivian, "and my wife and her business partner."

Charles's smile widened when he saw Vivian, and he moved to take her hand before bringing it to his lips.

"A pleasure, Mrs. Cross," Charles said.

"It's Malett, as I never took my husband's name," she corrected.

Charles raised an eyebrow, "You don't mean you are of the Dragmarsh Maletts?"

She smiled, casting an eye at Kaleb, "One and the same."

"Then I'm honored to have you on my ship, and I assure you the Gypsy Sky will not disappoint."

"Does she still have the Rebald Dual Core?" Tolbert asked.

Charles broke away from Vivian and eyed Tolbert, his gaze lingering on the scarf around the mage-tech's neck.

"It does, and I've also managed to add a Broker Fire-Funnel," he answered.

Tolbert frowned, "But the Broker would overload the Dual system, as the Rebald uses a water core," he said.

"Not this one. It is an Arcanian modification, the Rebald being converted to a fire core for greater longevity," Charles replied.

Tolbert's face brightened, "Then this was an old mail carrier, one of the Southern Longwings!"

"You know your airships," Charles said.

"Am I missing something?" Kaleb asked.

Tolbert stepped up, "During the early days of the Final War, the Arcanians were fighting on two fronts and needed to get supplies to both of them from a great distance. To achieve that, they designed a number of their ships with extremely long range while also supporting weighty payloads. As the war grew more pitched, and resources dwindled, the ships, known as Southern Longwings, were repurposed as bombers, but because they couldn't handle well. They were destroyed in droves until they were finally taken off active duty and those that remained were used to carry mail to soldiers on the lines."

"Interesting, but how does that help us?" Stoneham asked.

"It should allow us a great deal of range for exploration to the East, assuming what I was told last night was true," Charles answered.

"It is," Kaleb said.

Outside, the sound of running feet could be heard approaching the door, and both Parish and Greylin drew back on either side as a shadow appeared.

Kaleb's hand fell to his revolver, but the man in the frame was gasping and shaking his head with such fervor there was no way he could be a threat.

"Captain Cross," the man heaved out the words, "Your crew told me where I could find you, and I feared I'd be too late."

"Brett?" Kaleb asked.

The young noble nodded and stepped inside, his back covered in a heavy pack and his face running with lines of perspiration.

"What's this?" Vivian asked.

Kaleb smiled, "It would seem to be the last member of our company."

CHAPTER FIVE

SKYLLA

The torture of this is something I must use to my benefit, and only now can I fully understand what Kaleb must have felt when he knew I was with Ethran. Vivian Malett gives me focus, and with her among the crew I know my mind will stay keen as I can't afford to let her past my guard, both for my sake and that of Kaleb.

The *Gypsy Sky* had no plank. Instead a rope ladder hung from one of three openings in the ship's side. Skylla watched as those from the *Sand Tyger* climbed upward, and two young men, both greasy and in coveralls helped load Vivian and McBrayer's luggage from ropes dropped from a secondary opening.

"Do you like her?" Charles asked.

He was smiling again, and his levity helped keep a deep frown on her lips.

"When I met you at the *Barrel*, I knew you were down on your luck, but until I saw this ship I had no idea," she replied.

Laughing, he offered to take her position at the bottom of the rope ladder so she could climb.

"Well, I know she's not your typical ship, but in this day and age, what is typical in the sky is that fewer and fewer ships can rise into it," he said.

She took a step on the first wooden board and paused, saying, "It is the fault of your people that these ships no longer rise into the sky, and as long as you continue to turn your back on magic, then your society will continue to crumble."

Charles shrugged, "Well, that is for smarter men than me to decide, but until then, I'll use what I've learned to keep flying."

She eyed his neck, and there, beneath his leather apron and sweat-stained undershirt was a crimson scarf, the golden runes on it barely visible in the grime.

"You're a Mage-Tech," she said.

He nodded, "Yes, as any good Sky Captain should be if he wants to keep his bird aloft, and now that I see your hair, and the bands at your neck and wrists, I know you are no Samaya, so magic is in you."

"I've Enlightened blood, it's true," she replied.

His smile broadened, "Then I'm well met twice, as you're the first I've seen up close."

She stepped up another rung, but then paused and looked back down at him.

"What do you mean, 'up close'?" she asked.

"Well, I lost a ship two years ago beyond the central mountains of Aflyr, and it was the Enlightened that brought it down."

"How can you be sure?"

He sighed, "When you face an elemental storm, you can feel the magic in the air. I lost a good crew, and a good captain in that attack, some of them vaporized by lightning and others cast into the sky like dolls to be torn apart by the winds."

"You mean you weren't the captain?"

For a moment he stared out into space, but then snapped back and shook his head, "No, I was a junior Mage-Tech, Miss, and my father was the captain."

"I'm sorry," she offered.

His smile returned, and he shrugged, "I made peace with it, and it wasn't you who was responsible for that storm, so you've no reason to be sorry."

"True, but I have to wonder, Mr. Rutledge. After what happened, why would you ever want to go back?" she asked.

"Those at the *Barrel* would say for revenge, but my father and I had a dream, and I mean to see it done."

"And what dream is that?"

"A dozen years ago, when I was just fifteen, my father and I took a flite from his ship and while we flew, a woman appeared in the clouds.

She was the most beautiful thing either of us had ever seen, and we made a promise that if we could, we'd find a way to discover her and both propose marriage, let the better man win."

Skylla shook her head, "That seems a far-fetched promise."

Charles shrugged, "Well, you didn't see her because she was worth a fool's quest, and she flew east toward the mountains and the sea beyond."

"The Madras," Skylla said.

"Yes, and two years ago I saw that cursed inland sea for a moment before the storm struck. It was like a blanket of cobalt spread about emerald isles and towers of golden sunlight."

"That doesn't sound much like a place of curses," she said.

"Exactly, and I think the Enlightened want us to believe it is cursed so they can keep it to themselves."

"Well, I guess we'll all get to find out soon enough," she said.

He nodded, and she continued to climb, Parish waiting for her at the top of the ladder with an offered hand.

Tolbert and Charles were huddled together with the two man crew of the *Gypsy Sky*, one of the engine pods the source of their conversation. Skylla leaned against a rail and studied the chains that held the ship in place.

If there was a girl in the clouds, then perhaps more of Ethran's people are alive, but a part of me doesn't want that to be true. How callous have I become, then, to wish the end of my own people.

"Tolbert thinks we'll be airborne in another half an hour," Stoneham said.

She didn't turn, and continued to stare at the chains.

"Are they so interesting?" he asked.

"What?"

He pointed, "The chains."

Sighing she shook her head, "I was thinking of being tethered to a place you didn't belong, and how much this ship must need the sky."

"You make it sound like it's alive," he said.

"Maybe it is, in a way, or at least the magic bound into it is alive with purpose."

He scratched his sideburns, "I guess I never thought of it like that."

There was a protracted pause and then he continued, "Are you thinking about what it would be like without those bonds?"

If you only knew I'd put them on willing, perhaps you wouldn't ask...

"No, I understand my place in the world, and I know what the power they withhold can do to me."

"But do you ever wonder..." he broke off.

She turned, "Wonder what?"

"I don't know, that if you found someone like you, one of your people, they could teach you how to wield your power properly?"

She shook her head, "Stoneham, you are something else."

Smiling, he pretended to tip his cap, "As you say."

Going back to looking at the chain, she continued, "And no, I've not thought of that as those like me are a dying breed."

"Perhaps here on the coasts, but everyone knows that the further inland you go, the stranger the world and the more likely one is to find the Enlightened."

"Or maybe those are governments of the Great Five filling the minds of their people with false danger so they stay docile and cling to the industry they are hoping to build."

"Now you are talking like the captain," Stoneham said.

She was about to reply when the sound of an engine pod coming to life drowned out all else. Air whipped around her and she held her hair in check. Tolbert and the others excitedly clapped each other on the back.

"Looks like it was less time than he expected!" Stoneham shouted over the wind.

She nodded, and pointed inside the ship. Stoneham returned the nod and they both slipped inside, the gale abating as they closed the metal door.

Further down the interior passage Tolbert and Charles entered as well, removing their goggles with bright smiles on their faces.

Kaleb stepped from a room along that hall, as did his wife further down, and Charles called down to everyone, "We've ignited the engines and will be casting off. I suggest everyone find a place to buckle in until we've reached a navigable height."

"Well, you heard the man," Stoneham said.

She nodded, and watched as Kaleb returned to his quarters, then Vivian to hers. Once the hall was clear, she slipped down it and entered Kaleb's cabin without a knock.

He'd removed his hat and coat and was taking a seat on a fold-down bench with shoulder straps attached to it.

"Skylla?" he asked.

She slid into the seat next to him, kissed him full on the lips, and then began to strap herself in. He stared at her a moment before doing the same.

"What was that?" he asked.

"It was for a safe flight, and because I know what I have and don't intend to lose it."

The words came out without a pause, and only after speaking did she feel the sting of heat in her cheeks, but when Kaleb laughed she managed to smile.

"Well, then I'm glad I brought you after all, as it would be a very lonely voyage without you beside me."

Outside, the sound of chains falling to the stone beneath the ship echoed up into the superstructure. The craft listed to a side, and Kaleb was thrown against her, his weight only slightly supported by the straps. After a moment, the list straightened out, and he turned to her.

"A safe flight indeed," he said.

They both shared a laugh as the engines cycled up and the ship moved backward out of the rear of the hanger.

The *Gypsy* drifted high above the scattered green and grey landscape of the nation of Aflyr, ruins dotting the land like anthills, and Skylla watched each one from the observation deck with morbid interest.

A night and day in the sky and I feel thin, the smell of the ocean long gone in the west…

Outside, on one of the walkway's, Lance, one of the ship's two crewmen, fought against the wind as he secured a metal flashing that had come loose during the journey. She watched him at work, the man using a cable tether that went through loops at his shoulders as he inched out on a support to get to the broken sheet. He was dressed in heavy coveralls, his mustache whipping in the wind, and he had a canister gun in a hip holster and a helmet and goggles wrapped tightly around his head.

One false move and it would be the end if that rope tether snaps, and yet he works as though his feet were on the ground…

Lance continued his course, and she let her gaze drift to the horizon until a small shape appeared to move against it. She paused, squinting, and then saw it again, a bit of shadow among low clouds to the south.

What are you now?

Several minutes passed as she watched the shape, her stomach churning as the shadow took sharper form.

It draws closer…

Breaking away from the window, she moved from the observation deck into the ship's interior, then up a stair to the bridge. There, Kaleb leaned against a rail looking east, and Charles leaned into a chair while Paul, the other crewmen of the *Gypsy Sky*, held the wheel.

"Captain," she said.

Both Charles and Kaleb turned, and she winced before shaking her head.

"Sorry, Captain Rutledge, have you seen the shape to the south?" she asked.

Charles rose from his seat, and Kaleb moved along the rail until he was looking south as well, his field glasses lifted from his neck to his eyes.

"She's right," Kaleb said, "There's another ship out there."

Charles drew a spyglass from his apron and took a look as well.

"A Calico Interceptor?" Kaleb asked.

"No, I think it's a Brummon Skylord," Charles corrected.

"She has colors, a black saber on an orange field," Kaleb offered.

Charles removed his spyglass and sighed.

"What is it?" Skylla asked.

"Pirates," he replied.

"Do you have guns?" Kaleb asked.

Charles nodded, "Two, and we have a Torpedo Flit, but it won't fly without a Mage-Tech."

"Then you can fly it?" Kaleb asked.

Charles shook his head, "Not while I'm needed here. The primary elemental coil runs beneath the bridge, and, if we are in combat, I'll have to be here, channeling to the coil for maneuverability."

Kaleb turned to Skylla, "Right, then you get Stoneham and both of you man the guns, I'll find Tolbert and see about the Flit."

"Yes, Captain," she replied.

"How much time?" Kaleb asked.

Charles looked back at the growing shape on the horizon, "Ten, maybe fifteen minutes."

"Go!" Kaleb ordered.

Skylla turned and raced back down the stairs, her boots clanking against the metal runners until she struck the wood of the passenger deck. Once there, she raced along the doors, several of them open, until she found Stoneham's room.

The Quartermaster lay with his floppy green hat over his head, and Parish and Greylin played a game of dice at a small table across from the cots.

"Stoneham, we've got trouble," she said.

All eyes turned to her, Stoneham rising from his sleeping position with a disconcerted grunt.

"What is it?" Parish asked.

In the hall, the same question was echoed by Vivian Malett who had exited her room.

"Pirates, and Captain wants us on the ship's guns," she replied.

"Pirates!" Parish said, his verve matched the smile spreading across his face.

"Don't get too excited, kid. It ain't like the stories," Stoneham offered.

"How many?" Vivian asked.

Skylla didn't turn to the woman, but replied, "Just one ship, but they look well-armed."

"Pirates usually are," Stoneham said.

All three members of the crew moved out into the hall, McBrayer and Brett Bozeman having also come out of their cabins.

"You should stay in your cabin, Miss Malett," McBrayer said.

Vivian nodded, her pale face having lost even more color, and McBrayer ushered her from the hall as the rest of those gathered moved in opposite directions.

"I've got the Starside," Stoneham said.

"I'll take Groundside, and Parish you're with me," Skylla replied.

"What about me?" Brett asked.

"You should keep your head down, Mr. Bozeman, as bullets have an odd way of bouncing about cans like this," Stoneham called before he and Greylin disappeared up a stair at the end of the hall.

Skylla didn't have time to see the young man's reaction, Instead she slid down a ladder at mid-hall with Parish right behind her.

CHAPTER SIX

KALEB

I'm a sailor by trade, a man of the sea, and how I find myself drifting through the currents of the sky like a damnable gull is beyond me.

Kaleb found Tolbert in the coil room, the mage-tech scrawling down notes on a pad attached to the leg of his insulated coveralls as he poured over the engine.

"Mr. Tolbert, I'm going to need you," he called over the din of the coil.

Tolbert turned, placed a hand to his ear and yelled, "What?"

Marching forward, Kaleb grabbed him by the collar and pulled him from the room.

"Rutledge says there is a torpedo flit on this ship. Do you know where it is?" Kaleb asked once they were clear of the coil.

"Sure, Captain. It's attached in the aft hold. Why?"

"Because you're going to have to pilot it."

"What?"

"We've got trouble, and only a mage-tech can take one of those ships up."

Tolbert shook his head, "But Captain, flites are notoriously dangerous, and most don't work at all, as they are just put on ships to make sailors feel like they have an escape route, even if it is false hope."

Kaleb began marching aft, "Then we'd better hope this one will actually fly."

"Captain!" Tolbert followed after him,

"Yes?"

"I've never flown a flite before. I mean, I never even *saw* a flite before yesterday!"

"And how does this one look?"

"Well, I don't know… good I guess, but still, does it even have any functional cores?"

"Rutledge didn't indicate one way or the other, but he brought it up, so that must mean it works to some degree."

They moved quickly, a ladder and a portal passing along their course before they made it to the aft hold. It was a small chamber, lined with cables and chains, a single craft suspended from four clamps directly in the middle.

"It looks like a hammerhead shark," Kaleb said,

"The front wings are for steering, supposedly," Tolbert replied.

The mage-tech moved beneath the craft, his hand running along its belly as he closed his eyes.

"Anything?" Kaleb asked.

"I'd like to lie and say no, but there is an air core in the housing," Tolbert replied.

Kaleb nodded, "Then let's get to it."

Tolbert went to the wall where a collection of gears were located and released a catch. Grabbing a wheel-release, he started spinning it until there was a hiss of air that turned into a torrent as the back of the ship opened to the sky. Kaleb grabbed one of the chains and held on, the air sucking at his coat, and his hat tumbling off only to be caught by the strap around his neck.

"You'll have to climb aboard, Captain, and I'll join you once we are fully open!" Tolbert yelled.

Kaleb nodded and stepped out on the last remaining edge of metal that led beneath the craft as Tolbert waited. It was precarious climb, but he managed it, and finally pulled himself up into the thin ship.

There were two seats, one forward with levers and other navigation equipment and one further after that housed a swivel machine gun. Both were open to the air, and he adjusted his hat behind his back, pulled up his goggles, and then got into the weapons blister.

Tolbert was making the precarious climb himself, and once he got aboard he slipped into the pilot's seat and grabbed a leather helmet with two large pads at the ears. He pulled it on, then motioned to Kaleb who searched around below his seating well until he found a similar piece of equipment.

The leather was supple, and had a bit of fur lining in it with a buckle chinstrap and a single cable that led from one ear to the inner wall of the ship. He pulled it on, adjusted the strap, and suddenly a distant but audible relay of Tolbert's voice came into his right ear.

"Can you hear me, Captain?" Tolbert asked,

"Yes," he replied.

"These are flight relay helmets, and there is a sound stone in the strap that picks up vibrations from your throat when you speak and sends it along the cable to me," Tolbert said.

"Got it."

"Good, now if you worship a saint, I'd say it's time to do your praying," Tolbert said.

Banished Gods, I wish I did have a saint to give my prayers...

Tolbert reached out, grabbed a metal release, depressed the thumb lever and then pulled. There was a shudder followed by an instant of pause, then the ship slipped backward and into the sky.

Kaleb held his breath, the world dipping dangerously below them as Tolbert threw levers in front of him. Nausea rose in his throat, and the craft started to spin before there was a shudder, like the hand of a giant grabbing hold of them. Suddenly, they were righted in alignment to the horizon.

"Well what do you know. It works," Tolbert said.

Kaleb fought down the bile and then looked around, the *Gypsy Sky* floating a hundred feet above them and to the south, the dark interloping ship now much closer than the last time he'd seen it.

"They are getting close," he said.

"Copy that. Should we take a look?" Tolbert asked.

Kaleb checked the gun, a chain of ammunition hanging from it that led to a box near his feet. He primed it, turned the barrel away from Tolbert's head, which was precariously close when he faced the weapon fore, and then squeezed the trigger.

The barrel pushed up and a series of rounds, some touched with phosphorous, spit out into the sky.

"Yeah, we're good, so let's give these newcomers a look," Kaleb replied.

Tolbert nodded, the front guide-wings tilting as he turned the ship toward the oncoming pirate.

The pirate vessel was smaller than the *Sky Gypsy*, but not by much. She was a twin-hull craft with lift gas stowed in long metal cylinders over each pontoon. Three engines drove her, and several weapons' blisters could be seen twinkling in the daylight at their approach.

"She's well-armed," Kaleb said.

"True, Captain, but we've got two torpedoes, so don't discount what we can do," Tolbert replied.

The flash of a machine gun erupted on the pirate vessel, and Tolbert jinked the craft as Kaleb ducked.

"Well, so much for a show of force dissuading them," Kaleb said.

There was return fire from the *Gypsy Sky*, and Kaleb turned to see twin weapon blisters, one topside and one below, firing duel-mounted guns on a swivel similar to that of the flit.

"We can't stay between them," Tolbert said.

Kaleb nodded, but Tolbert had already begun a climb, the wind rushing past in a constant wave. The flit's nose rose up and up before the battle was lost as Kaleb hung on.

"We are going back, right?" Kaleb asked.

As if on cue, Tolbert turned the ship back and down, the nose falling and Kaleb being thrown forward as vertigo made his head spin, both the pirate and *Gypsy Sky* coming into view far beneath them.

The two ships were exchanging fire, and the enemy vessel was falling back.

The pirate is trying to get behind them so he can then come up beside for boarding or...

Between the pontoons, Kaleb spied something, and he reached into his coat for his field glasses. The flit continued to fall, and he had a hard time finding the pirate in his vision, but when he did, he hissed a curse.

"She's got a rocket cluster!" he shouted.

"If they get behind the *Gypsy*, they might just decide to bring her down and pick at the wreckage," Tolbert said.

"Can you fire a torpedo?" Kaleb asked.

"I can try," Tolbert said.

"Do it."

The ship turned slightly, and Tolbert reached to a lever on his right, pulled it back and then hit a release. Beside Kaleb the front of a tube opened and the nose of torpedo was primed in the cylinder.

"At this range I'm not sure..."

"Just do it!" Kaleb yelled.

Tolbert pushed a button on his control panel and there was a burst of heat as the torpedo left the cylinder. Kaleb shielded his face with his arm and then leaned out as the smoke trail raced from the flit toward the pirate.

Below, spotters waved on the enemy vessel, and it pitched away, the torpedo sailing past as it rocketed toward earth.

"Sorry, Captain, but like I said, we were too far out."

"No, Mr. Tolbert, we did what we had to do," Kaleb replied.

The pirate had lost the advantage, Captain Rutledge having taken the opportunity to turn away from the pursuit as his guns spat bullets all along the nose of the enemy craft. Windows shattered and smoke rose from the enemy ship's starboard.

"Take us closer. I want to be sure it doesn't recover," Kaleb said.

Tolbert aimed the flit into another dive. The air ripped from Kaleb's lungs before the ship evened out and the enemy vessel came into full view before them. It was huge, and as they came toward it one of the gun blisters opened up on them.

Bullets ripped around the flit, a few finding purchase along the port side and in the front wing, but then they were through and streaking along the ship's side. Kaleb turned his own gun and pulled the trigger, rounds zipping between the ships as he left a pock-marked scar all along one side before they were clear.

"Take us in for another pass!"

Tolbert started their bank, and more fire followed them but they were too hard to lead until once again they only showed the enemy their nose which made for another daunting target. Kaleb huddled down and found a new belt of ammunition, pulling the near spent one from his weapon and replacing it with the new. He'd completed the reload just as the dark shape of the pirate loomed before them once more.

This time the enemy missed completely, and Kaleb dumped another half a belt into the ship, killing a crewman trying to align a rifle shot from an exterior rail as well as smoking one of the ship's three engines.

Still, the pirate had managed to once again threaten the aft of the *Gypsy*, and Kaleb ordered another pass.

"Tolbert, align us for our second torpedo!"

"That's a hard shot, Captain," Tolbert replied.

"What's our best chance?"

"Come in from above and behind, but that exposes us to their topside battery, and I'm not sure we'll survive that."

Kaleb eyed the two ships and sighed.

"We've got to make sure the Gypsy makes it, so take us in!"

Tolbert nodded and Kaleb hunkered down into the well and reached into his coat. In the left breast was the stock for his pistol, and he withdrew it and then pulled his repeater from its holster at his hip. His fingers were quick, attaching the stock and then reaching into his left breast for the scope he kept there.

He locked the scope atop the pistol, checked the alignment with his scratched presets, and then stood.

The pirate was just in sight beneath the nose of the craft, and he wedged himself in beside the machine-gun, bringing the modified pistol to his shoulder.

"Give me a shot if you can!"

Tolbert looked back over his shoulder, then back at the enemy.

"Right!"

Kaleb brought his eye to the scope, the bulk of the pirate's topside coming into view as he watched the magically laced rangefinder shift at their approach.

1000 yards, 900, 800, 700...

Machine-gun fire sounded above the cry of the wind, and Tolbert jinked the craft as bullets blazed past.

"Steady!"

500, 400...

Several rounds found purchase in the ship's nose, but the reinforced ram there deflected most, a stray round creasing Tolbert's shoulder but he held the course.

Kaleb focused on the gunner, the man wearing goggles and laughing as he blazed away with his quad guns.

300, 200...

Kaleb fired a single round, and the machine-gun went silent.

"You're clear," Kaleb said.

Tolbert tipped the lit downward another notch and primed the second torpedo, this one to Kaleb's right. At fifty yards Tolbert released the torpedo and it sped out and down just as the flit banked away from incoming small arms fire.

Kaleb leaned out of the well and caught a glimpse of the torpedo as it sped into the bridge cluster between the pontoons. When it struck, the explosion was massive, and a ball of fire split the pontoons, both sides of the ship tumbling down trailing smoke and debris into the air.

"Nice shot," Kaleb said.

"Not bad yourself, Captain," Tolbert replied.

Kaleb smiled as Tolbert pulled the flit around and angled it behind the *Gypsy Sky*. Smoke was trailing from one of the ship's engines, and there was noticeable damage to the superstructure, but otherwise she continued on her easterly course.

Let's hope that is our only such encounter this trip…

To his right, he caught movement in the clouds, but when he turned there was nothing there.

But I probably couldn't be that lucky…

"I'll take it from here, Captain," Tolbert said.

The flit hung from the moorings, and Tolbert was busy making sure each connection was secure. Lance, one of the ship's crew, had come down to direct them back into the hold, and once inside Kaleb had broken down his gun after helping with the stowing.

"Good work out there," Kaleb said.

Tolbert turned and nodded, the tear in his jacket from a stray round sticking up oddly at the shoulder.

"Thanks," the young mage-tech replied.

Kaleb nodded, and moved to the door where he was greeted by Skylla. Her hair was windblown and the sulfuric scent of gunpowder clung heavily to her.

"That was damn foolish, Captain," she said.

He drew his hat from where it hung on the strap at his neck and replaced it on his head.

"Sometimes foolish is the only way to get the job done," he replied.

She was about to say something else when Vivian pushed past her and threw her arms around Kaleb's neck.

"What the!" he said.

She smelled of honeyed perfume, and she held him in a lasting embrace.

Banished Gods she's light, I'd forgotten what it was like to hold her...

"Why must you vex me so with your daredevil deeds?" she whispered.

"Viv, really, it's part of the job," he said.

She pulled back enough to look him straight in the eye.

"You always were the hero. It's why I fell in love with you," she said.

He gulped, and the smell of the ocean overpowered the perfume. Skylla marched off down the hall, and he tried to break away from Vivian but she held firm to his neck, forcing his eyes back to hers.

"Why are you doing this?" he asked.

She stared at him, her eyes dark and searching before she finally sighed and let herself fall back to the deck.

"I'm sorry," she said.

He rolled his eyes, "Viv, you can't be serious."

Straightening her dress, she tuned to go. "I guess I forget what we are sometimes, especially when you save my life."

"Viv..."

She raised a hand over her shoulder with a curt wave and slipped away, Kaleb standing alone in the hall shaking his head.

I'd almost have preferred getting shot down...

CHAPTER SEVEN

SKYLLA

It makes my skin crawl to see her touch him, and yet somehow I'm the one who is in the wrong. What kind of cruel hand of fate is that, where the man I love is married to a woman who may still love him as well?

If she doesn't, she certainly plays at it well enough. And yet she was the one who held him, thanked him, told him she loved him while I simply called him foolish.

I've known I don't deserve him, especially after what I did with Ethran, and yet I'd deny a woman, his wife, the right to be with him when I'm not even capable of showing him how I feel freely and from the heart.

Saint Shera, help me find a way to make this right... even if right means stepping aside...

Skylla hung in the air, cable strapped to a harness around her torso and a hose in her hands. Lance was near her, his eyes covered with shielded glasses while he used a blue-flamed torch to seal a breach in the hull.

Somewhere above the crew went about its business, but she held herself against the ship's frame and tried to avoid looking directly at the torch.

I'd rather be in the open air than up there with the rest as I swear a part of me wants to strangle Vivian each time I come in contact with her...

Lance moved, and she followed, both of them swinging precariously as he went about further repairs. He'd been patching holes and checking damage for two hours, and her cheeks were wind-burned and the harness had cut deeply into her but she stayed close, never complaining.

Below, she watched the open expanses of ruin turn into foothills, virgin forests spilling out over them as the world turned from ash to emerald.

It looks like there were some places the war didn't touch, at least while looking from this height…

Lance finished a weld and turned the torch off, yelling, "I think that's it, Ma'am!"

She nodded with tight lips and then pulled the guide cable three times. In moments they were both being lifted up into the ship, Kaleb the first to greet them.

"How did it go?" he asked.

She didn't reply, but shrugged a shoulder at Lance who took off his goggles with a sigh, answering, "As good as could be expected, but I can't get close to the tanks with this."

He held up the extinguished torch, and Kaleb nodded.

"Captain Rutledge wants to see us on the bridge," he said.

"Both of us?" Skylla asked.

"Yes, unless you're too tired from the self-imposed work below," he replied.

Her cheeks burned, but she managed to nod, "No, I'm fine."

Removing the harness and shaking blood back into her lower half, she followed Kaleb as he made his way forward. He didn't talk along the way, and she drifted behind him instead of at his side, her eyes trailing over his back.

When they reached the bridge, Stoneham, McBrayer, and Vivian were already there with Charles seated in his command chair. When she and Kaleb entered, he nodded and got to his feet.

"Good, and how did the repairs go?" Charles asked.

"Fine, at least as far as I could tell," Skylla replied.

He gave her that unsuppressed smile and then walked to a series of controls near the steering column. Tapping on a gauge, he sighed, and then turned his attention back to those gathered.

"Well, the good news is that we survived the attack and the ship is intact. The bad news, however, is that our lift gas is leaking, and we've no way to fix the tanks," Charles said.

"What does that mean?" Vivian asked.

Skylla kept her gaze away from the woman like she had the torch, instead looking at Kaleb. He was adjusting his hat with brow furrowed.

"What it means, Ms. Malett, is that we'll slowly descend until we are forced to land, and we'll never clear the mountains."

"I wouldn't be too sure about that," McBrayer said.

Charles shook his head, "Rest assured, Mr. McBrayer, I've done the calculations and…"

The captain trailed off, his eyes following those of McBrayer out the port window. Skylla turned as well and sucked in a quick breath when she saw the shape in the clouds.

"What is that?" Stoneham asked.

"Honestly, I have no idea," Charles whispered.

There, suspended in the air like a child's toy, was a settlement. A dozen houses and half that number of towers were set on a collection of rune-covered stone pillars, while walkways, bridges, and even a twisting aqueduct connected the various dwellings.

"That's impossible," Vivian said.

"You'd be surprised what is possible once you leave the cities of the Samaya," Kaleb replied.

Skylla heard the words, but her skin was alive with sensation, and as she watched, people appeared on the walkways, several of them taking flight toward the wounded *Gypsy Sky*.

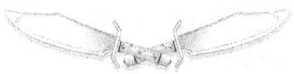

The ship was guided into a birth by three men and a woman, all of whom swam in the air like it was an ocean. Skylla saw a bit of Ethran in each one, skin deep chocolate, hair dark, and eyes bright blue like the open sky.

At the berth, a short man with skin like granite, bat-winged ears, and a set of tinted goggles on his bald hairless head tied up the ship as children gathered close behind several men in ancient armor and bright spears.

"This is insanity," Stoneham said.

Brett Bozeman had forced his way to the front of the craft, white-knuckled hands on the rail and eyes scanning the settlement.

"I assure you, Mr. Stoneham, the Enlightened are real, I just never knew they could do this," Brett offered.

Stoneham rolled his eyes, "I'm not saying the Enlightened don't exist. I mean I need look no further than Skylla to tell me that. All I'm saying is that towns in the sky shouldn't be possible."

"Magic makes anything possible," Skylla whispered.

Before anyone could reply, a man in deep burgundy robes and holding a white marble-topped walking cane moved past the children and guards toward the end of the berth. Kaleb and Charles both stood at the ship's plank, Lance extending it down to the dock, but the newcomer did not take it. Instead, he waited, stroking his grey beard and eventually Kaleb walked down to meet him.

Skylla watched the two speak. Several times both of them looked back at her until she was waved down to join them. She moved through the crew, Brett hard at her heels, but when they got to the plank, Charles stopped the archeologist from going further, and Skylla walked down alone.

"Skylla, I'd like you to meet Greysemmer, Town Captain of Skywatch," Kaleb said.

The older man smiled and offered a small bow, his eyes avoiding her wristbands and choker.

"Well met, Skylla. We are greatly pleased to have one of our own return to us here in the clouds," he said.

Kaleb's face tightened, but Skylla nodded, saying, "My home is with those who raised and protected me, Mr. Greysemmer. I've no more place in the clouds than a dolphin on land."

The man nodded, "It is just Greysemmer, and I understand your way of thinking, but nonetheless, a dolphin is a mammal just like a bear or the household cat, and they all breath the same air of the surface world, even if the dolphin has forgotten what it is like to live on the land."

"As you say," she replied.

"Yes, well, Greysemmer has just made an offer to let us stay on Skywatch until our ship can be repaired," Kaleb said.

Skylla raised an eyebrow, asking Greysemmer, "And why would you do that?"

"You may be from the cities of the Samaya, but the war was not our cause, and we have no ill will to anyone as we live in peace away from the rest of the world," Greysemmer answered.

"That may be, but now that this ship knows you are here..." she began.

Greysemmer raised a hand, "Do you think we are bound to the earth like a Samaya village? No, dear girl, we may travel the winds, so knowing we are here and finding us are two different things, as we have proven since the final days of the war."

She had no reply for that, and Kaleb broke in, "Then we would be very grateful for your assistance."

Greysemmer nodded and offered Skylla his hand. She looked at Kaleb, but he tipped his head and she reached out.

The contact was like touching a skillet left too long on a stove, and she withdrew her fingers instantly and rubbed her hand. Greysemmer staggered, but regained his balance with the help of his cane. Further up the dock people murmured, and the guards took a step closer but the old man held up a hand.

"I apologize," he said, "I wasn't prepared for that."

"Prepared for what?" Kaleb demanded.

"I am a Human, a being of the eternal flame, but in all my years I've never touched the deep water of a Wizard, and our opposition threw me a moment."

Kaleb turned to Skylla who still rubbed her hand, the bands on her wrists and neck aching almost as much as her stinging fingers.

"Come," Greysemmer said. "We would show you the hospitality of the Enlightened."

The older man moved back up the dock, and Kaleb drew close to her, words whispered beneath the shield of his mustache.

"These people can't be trusted," he said.

"I know," she replied.

And this time, I mean that...

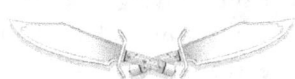

The town rose up around Skylla in three layers, the first a series of giant disks of stone supported by rune-inscribed pillars; the second small houses and lattice-suspended gardens; and the last a collection of three-story towers that were set in the central ring of each foundation stone. Bridges connected all the towers, and, below, more bridges connected the foundation stones, the entire community taking on the aspect of a spider's web suspended in the clouds.

People watched the procession from the ship, led by Kaleb, as they followed the guards and Greysemmer across a windswept bridge onto a stone where water cascaded down to a central pool from a smooth-stoned tower of the island.

Behind Kaleb, Brett walked with a journal in hand as he tried to sketch what he saw. Then came Stoneham and Parish, all others having stayed behind with the injured *Gypsy*.

Children walked behind them, having broken away from their mothers' grips, and they cautiously came forward almost close enough to touch the strangers before rushing back to their friends with giggles.

These people seem at peace, and the presence of children speak to a future I didn't think was possible...

"I think the tower is our destination," Kaleb whispered.

She looked up, the structure seemingly larger as they drew close, and the sound of the water bringing gooseflesh to her skin.

"I still don't believe what I'm seeing," she replied.

"Incredible," Brett broke in. "The professors at university will never believe this."

"I'd guess that is exactly what these people hope in bringing us here, that no one in their right mind would believe us," Parish said.

"Either that or they don't ever intend for us to leave," Stoneham offered.

It's always nice that you don't pull your punches, Stoneham, because I know that's what I was feeling too...

The waterfall actually broke over a stone canopy, the water spraying down on either side, leaving an entry open that led to a set of double doors. Skylla reached up and touched the mist that gently fell around the entrance, the water beading on her fingers and the smell intoxicating.

Greysemmer turned once he reached the doors, his face pale amid the mists. "This is as far as most of you may go, although we have prepared a meal and rooms for you all in the garden surrounding the tower."

"Most of us?" Kaleb asked.

"Yes, only one with Elemental blood may pass these doors," Greysemmer replied.

Kaleb shook his head, but Skylla put a hand on his arm, "Don't worry, Captain. Enjoy the meal, and I'm sure I'll be back with you shortly, yes?"

She turned back to Greysemmer at that last, and he nodded, "You are always free to go wherever you like."

Kaleb sighed, but he relented, and the guards drew the rest of the company away toward the far side of the pool. Once they were out of earshot, Greysemmer spoke again.

"Would you be so kind?" he asked, waving at the door.

Skylla furrowed her brow, "What?"

"I would ask that you open the door," he continued.

The hairs on the back of her neck stood on end. *What is he up to?*

"It is a test, you see, as the doors will only open to an Enlightened, and thus I would see you open them instead of me," Greysemmer offered.

She looked up, the stone canopy above her head creating a half-circle of water around the flags at her feet. Beneath it the door was made of heavy wood set with honeyed-oricalcum bands covered in runes.

It is an important place...

"Is this your only water source?" she asked.

Greysemmer continued smiling, but the paleness in his cheeks had become sallow.

"No, water collects in cisterns on each island, why?"

"It is an odd thing, to have water come from the tower as if it is somehow generated in this place alone," she replied.

"A keen observation, and yes, this tower is one of our treasures, which is why I invited you to see it," he said.

"You mean open it," she corrected.

The man's smile faltered a bit, but he recovered with a chuff of a laugh.

"The outside world has made you untrusting, daughter of the deep," he said.

"No, interaction with liars, both Samaya *and* Enlightened, have made me untrusting," she replied.

Greysemmer swayed a bit and caught himself with his cane before wiping water from his brow.

"Are you well?" she asked, still standing well away from the door.

"No," he replied, "The water, I'm not used to it."

"You are Human?"

"Yes."

"Are their Corsairs among you, or Candon?" she asked.

He laughed, and settled down on the threshold, a sigh escaping his lips.

"No, we have no water-born on the islands," he answered.

She walked over to the curtain of falling water, extended her hand into it and closed her eyes. For a moment visions of the tower's creation sprang to her mind in a kaleidoscope of images, the most prevalent of which were an ancient woman with hair green as the far-sea Sargasso working alongside Kin as they lay each block that she sealed with a kiss of her magic.

Dreamlike reflection of the sky, the people here, and finally the green-haired woman resting in the tower's upper chambers assaulted her senses. At last a lone vision of the woman played out, her form unmoving as she reclined in a skeletal heap upon silk sheets. The image pulled at her and she jerked her hand from the water.

"What did you see, daughter of the deep?" Greysemmer asked.

"Your Wizard is dead," she replied.

He nodded, "It is as we had all feared for many more years than you can imagine, but now at last we know the truth of it."

"Who was she?"

"Her name was Iquia, and she was old even in the days of the opening of the Shining Cities during the 9th Age of Man," he answered.

"I'm sorry for your loss," she said.

"I thought I might have finally found a way inside this tower, but I was wrong not to tell you of my hope," he said.

"And why do you wish to enter so badly?" she asked.

"It is not the entry that matters to me. It is the soul who could open the tower. Iquia was our guide, our builder, our leader, and our faith. Without her, we've been adrift here, slowly sailing around the Madras and its reaches, but the winds have finally brought us into Aflyr, and if we continue West, we will leave the seclusion of the inland sea and the ships of the Samaya will find us, and..."

"Destroy you," she finished for him.

He nodded.

"What of your Aspara? Couldn't they guide you in the air currents?"

"Indeed, and the few who live among us have kept us in the Madras for four generations of Humankind, but a series of storms battered us this past year, and with each one we were pushed further into the world-flow, and I'm afraid the wind-magic of the Aspara can no longer keep us on our course, as this is no child's kite to be flitted about. The stones are hard to move, and resist the power of the air."

"And yet they fly?" she asked.

"Yes, and so you know the true power of Wizard-kind. The *afterglow* they bound to the pillars beneath us is enough to break the stone's will that longs to be deep in the earth, but only a Wizard can also pursue the stone to be moved against the wind, as it is now free to do as it pleases."

"You make it sound like the stone is alive."

"Perhaps it is. The Kin feel the stone whisper, or perhaps grumble, but they cannot bend it to their will either, as it is changed forever."

"Then you would have me speak to the stone?"

"If it is within your power."

She looked back at the door, her fingers rubbing against one another in anticipation as the bands at her neck and wrists burned.

"Step aside," she said.

Greysemmer's eyes widened, and he used his cane to rise and then walk away from the opening.

She moved forward, her feet on the threshold and a sense of power making her hair wet and her clothes heavy.

Looking down, she saw her skin shading to green, a fine webbing growing between her fingers.

"I've never seen such a thing," Greysemmer whispered.

"I'm not a Wizard," she replied.

I'm something else, or something more, but only half of me carries the line of the deep...

Reaching out, she placed her palm against the cool of the oricalcum, a shock of energy racing up her arm and exploding in her mind. She screamed, at least in her head, and her legs gave way as darkness wrapped her in a cloak so thick it smothered her in an instant.

"Daughter? Skylla? Can you hear me?"

She squeezed her eyes shut, a dull pain aching in every muscle in her body.

"Where?" she managed.

"You fell, but the door... you've opened it."

Blinking, she saw Greysemmer's weathered face above her, and beside him the now ajar double doors of Iquia's tower.

"Did you go inside?" she asked.

"No, it is not a place for any Human, at least not one wise enough to understand such things," he replied.

She tried to rise, but her head swam and Greysemmer helped her until she was upright. It was only then that the pain at her neck and wrists began to throb and she gritted her teeth.

"What is it?" he asked.

"The bands... there is something wrong," she said.

"What can I do?"

"Get Kaleb, he has the key."

Greysemmer nodded, got to his feet and moved from the canopy out into the daylight of the path. She rubbed the band at her neck, winced, but then stood up and turned to the entry.

The Afterglow is in me, more than the bands can stand...

Taking a single step, she drew closer to the threshold and smelled the sea beyond.

How is that possible? We are hundreds of miles from the depths...

Behind her, the sound of boots on the flags could be heard, and she turned away from the opening, but instead of Kaleb, it was a Kin who accompanied Greysemmer.

"Where is Kaleb?" she demanded.

"He is in the gardens with the rest of your company, but DireHammer was tending the stone on the verge, and he has some expertise with the slave bands," Greysemmer replied.

The Kin was short, no more than five feet, and his eyes were shielded with a grey-glass mask that tucked up around his bat-ears with a gold tie.

She was about to protest when pain struck her in a wave, the wrists and neck bands pulsing in conjunction with nerve deadening power.

"Please, daughter, let DireHammer help you," Greysemmer pleaded.

Kaleb...

Another wave struck, this one forcing a scream from her lips, and she fell to a knee. The Kin didn't wait for an answer, instead moving forward with sandstone-colored hands to place both palms on one of the bands at her wrist.

He began to hum, a low sound that rattled her bones, and his ears flattened on back against his head as he rocked to and fro. The band quivered, the runes blazing to life, and pain again struck before the sound of cracking metal echoed beneath the watery vault.

With a flash, the folds in the bands clicked and broke, the metal reluctantly heeding the earth-born's desire. He moved on to the other wrist, and after a moment it did the same. Both oricalcum bands steaming as they came away from her skin.

DireHammer then moved behind her and placed his palms on the choker, the thing hanging on a few seconds longer than the wrist bands before it too broke open and a shuddering breath slithered into her throat at the release.

I wasn't even aware I'd stopped breathing…

"Are you well, daughter of the deep?" DireHammer asked.

His voice was thick and melodic, like the harmony of a huge chime struck close to your chest.

"Yes… thank you," she managed.

"Should I still fetch your captain?" Greysemmer asked.

Skylla looked down at her naked wrists as a glow radiated from her fingers before turning back to the open door.

"No," she whispered, "It's better that he stay away for the moment."

DireHammer and Greysemmer exchanged a look but said nothing. Skylla got to her feet and once again faced the darkness of the open doorway.

CHAPTER EIGHT

KALEB

There are many times in life when you must trust your gut. It's not always easy to do, especially when your heart wants to get in the way.

Now I must trust my gut again, even if my mind continually races back to that tower and what it might mean for all of us as 'guests' of the people of this settlement in the sky…

The sun blazed down in shining pillars throughout the sheltered glade. Amid golden shafts, the sound of falling water and the twitter of small birds made a kind of music. Kaleb and the others sat beneath three small pavilions that surrounded the tower pool, the vegetation so lush that only the top of the tower was visible from their position.

Shielding his eyes, Kaleb looked up at it and gritted his teeth.

"She'll be fine," Stoneham said.

"I wish I had your confidence," Kaleb replied.

Brett, who was close by inspecting some inscriptions on a moss-covered monolith, turned to look at them as he adjusted his spectacles.

"Why would they wish to hurt her?" he asked.

"They wouldn't," Stoneham replied too quickly for Kaleb to answer.

Kaleb frowned and looked from the tower to the guards, all three of them wearing silvered chain hauberks, metal bracers and winged helmets. Their faces were placid, and yet he could feel the heat coming off them in subtle waves, each one keeping a hand on a rune-tipped spear and the hilt of a sword at their belts.

"Lowl," Brett said suddenly.

"What"? Stoneham asked.

Kaleb followed the archeologist's eyes to the path winding through the garden. Coming up the stone walk was a tall humanoid with a man's muscled body and the head similar in aspect and hair coloration to a canine.

Parish stood up, and Kaleb let his hand fall to the pistol at his hip, the guards tensing and the heat beneath the pavilion going up several degrees.

When the creature came under the shade of the pavilion, it raised its human-like hands, bowing slightly. "Greetings. We have prepared a meal for you, and I would ask that you accompany me to the observatory."

"Where's Skylla?" Kaleb asked.

"She's gone into the tower, and we cannot know when she will return as the elder has gone with her," he replied.

The inflection and pronunciation was off, his lips unable to curve like that of a man, and thus his accent made him seem even more exotic.

"Captain, I don't like this," Stoneham whispered.

The Lowl's long ears turned, and it was clear he could hear much better than those around him, something in the distance drawing his attention.

"We will accept your hospitality," Kaleb replied to the Lowl.

The creature bowed again, and then turned back down the path, the guards falling in behind the small company as they followed him. Brett moved forward until he was beside the creature, his eyes like two saucers as he smiled awkwardly.

"Might I ask you a question?"

The Lowl looked beside him, his head at least a foot taller than that of the thin archeologist.

"Yes."

"Is it true your sense of smell can detect a Samaya on the breeze from a quarter mile?"

The Lowl let his tongue come out and lick across his dark nose, the effect leaving a glistening film over the skin as he sniffed the air twice.

"More if the winds are right," the Lowl answered.

Brett, his journal still in hand, jotted down the reply, and the Lowl laughed.

"You record facts that no longer mean anything in this world," it said.

"I would have thought that true, until this morning when your town came into view," Kaleb said.

The Lowl looked over his shoulder, his spotted mane of hair creeping down his neck and into his shirt.

"We are the last, and it is only a matter of time now," the Lowl said.

"It's a big world, and the Enlightened are masters of finding ways to hide," Kaleb continued.

The Lowl didn't answer as they came to the bridge that connected the water tower to another island. Walking across it, Kaleb watched as birds played in the wind currents both below and above.

Brett finally broke in again as they approached a wooden structure that hung precariously off the side of this new island. "May I ask your name?"

"Hazra," The Lowl answered.

"It is nice to meet you," Brett continued.

Stoneham rolled his eyes, but Hazra nodded and offered the archeologist his hand. Kaleb almost spoke up, but instead held his tongue as Brett enthusiastically took it. The young man smiled heartedly for a second as he shook, then his eyes grew wide and he jerked his hand away with a yelp of pain.

"Sorry," Hazra let his tongue loll out, "The fire can get the better of me at moments like this."

You have full control, but you wanted to put Brett in his place, and for that I don't blame you…

Brett nodded as he rubbed his hand, and Hazra opened the door to the building and ushered them inside. The interior was a splendid display of carved stone with polished wood accents, the entry opening up to a lower chamber that was exposed to the sky. A stone and wood rail shielded the opening, and tables sat close to it to help facilitate a breathtaking view of the landscapes floating below.

A feast of fruits and vegetables was laid across the centermost table, and clay mugs with both water and a darker liquid were provided as well.

"We do not have much, but we hope this will sustain," Hazra said.

"We thank you for your hospitality," Kaleb replied.

Hazra nodded, and the party moved down the four steps to the lower platform, Parish going to the rail and the rest taking their seats.

"There's no meat," Stoneham said.

"No, but there is bread and honey," Brett offered.

"I don't trust vegetarians," Stoneham grumbled.

"I doubt very much that they are vegetarians, Mr. Stoneham, but living in a place like this would severely limit their ability to sustain slaughter animals, and the access to wild game would also be limited to whatever birds were worth the difficulty of hunting," Brett continued.

Stoneham shrugged, took a piece of warm bread and broke it as steam rose from the white interior.

"I saw a plot of wheat on one of the upper islands, and the houses here all grow gardens as every inch of space seems devoted to some kind of agriculture, even the rooftops," Parish added.

"They are a self-sustaining people, but nonetheless, there is a kind of leanness to this place, and that speaks of something we shouldn't trust," Kaleb said.

Stoneham nodded, and Parish came away from the rail to take a seat next to them.

"Do you have a plan?" Parish whispered.

"Not exactly, but I hope Charles is getting the Gypsy repaired because I have a bad feeling we'll be needing to get out of here much more quickly than we came in."

The rest of them looked back at the door, only the guards remaining, and then went about eating, the conversation minimal as each delved into his own inner thoughts.

Thunder rolled across the sky, and Kaleb adjusted his hat as the wind tore through the town. Hazra hadn't returned, but in his place a Kin came to take them to a building which was yet another island away from the water tower and four away from the Gypsy.

Like the building in which they ate, this one was open on one side to the sky, although the windows were less dramatic and the Kin rolled in wooden shutters as the first spattering drops of rain blew into from the darkening sky.

"I hope you will take a solid rest, and do not worry, the town has survived a thousand such storms without so much as a single shutter torn away," the Kin said.

"Again, we thank you for your hospitality," Kaleb said.

The Kin bowed and departed, the three guards outside the building putting on heavy cloaks, but Kaleb noted the same pale quality to their skin that Greysemmer had when he'd gone beneath the water tower.

"What do you make of this?" Stoneham asked.

"That we are slowly being moved further away from Skylla and our means of escape," Kaleb replied.

"Yeah, that was my thought too," Stoneham said.

Brett looked up from where he was sketching in his journal and Parish moved to press his ear against the door.

"Captain, these people have been nothing but hospitable," Brett said.

"And that is what's troubling me. You do understand our race is bent on their utter destruction?" Kaleb asked.

"Yes, that's been the case in the past, but with the war at an end…"

"Kid, you need to wake up! These people hate us, just as much as we hate them, and when they've gotten what they want, meaning Skylla, we'll be dealt with quickly," Stoneham said.

"But…"

Stoneham put his right boot on the table and produced a small revolver, checked the cylinder, and then moved toward the door.

"You still have those special rounds?" Stoneham asked.

"Two of them" Kaleb replied.

"But…" Brett said again.

"With the storm on us, and the night in full swing, we've probably got one shot at this, but we'll have to wait for a signal from Skylla," Kaleb said.

Parish went to the crank the Kin had used to close the shutters and gave it a turn, the panels opening slightly as wind a rain began to blow through. He went to the opening, looked out, and when he pulled back his hair was down and dripping into his eyes.

"Anything?" Stoneham asked.

"Nope, it is an overhang, and in this weather there is no way we could make a climb."

Kaleb nodded, "Then it is through the guards."

"Captain, you can't be serious!" Brett protested.

"I'm dead serious, Mr. Bozeman, and I suggest you keep yourself ready to move or we'll leave you here with these people you so admire," Kaleb said.

The young man blanched, looked at the faces staring back at him and then began to pack his journal in his leather satchel.

"Parish, can you get a view of the tower from the window?" Kaleb asked.

"Yes, but just barely," Parish replied.

"Good, then keep an eye there. Stoneham, we'll need those weapons, and I'll take the first shot, but you've got to get to the guard's spear before the others can react," Kaleb said.

"You can count on it," Stoneham replied.

Kaleb sighed and pulled a seat away from the wall so he could face the door as he loaded a runed round into his revolver.

Skylla, you've got to give us the word, and by the Banished Gods let's hope Charles has the Gypsy ready...

CHAPTER NINE

SKYLLA

I'm ever weary of my people, if they can truly be called that. I certainly share their blood, but the lineage and suffering of the Samaya is also carried in my veins. I take equal pride in both, although there is disappointment that each feels the need to use me for its own desperate purpose.

Now, I've got the chance to have some of my questions answered about exactly who I am, assuming the memories that this tower holds will help me where no other has been able to.

Skylla walked over the verge and the world shifted slightly at the edge of her vision. For a moment the interior looked like a desert mirage, wavy and distorted, but then it solidified until she stood in a grand foyer, twin staircases moving up into another level some fifty feet above.

"Impossible..." she whispered.

"No, nothing is impossible for the Wizards," Greysemmer said.

She turned. Greysemmer had come into the tower followed by DireHammer.

"The Wizards were able to bend space, making structures of impossible size inside a shell no larger than mundane homes or towers," Greysemmer said.

"How?" she asked.

"That is for those of the deep water to know," Greysemmer replied.

Frowning, she looked back to the stair, the marble runners on each step glistening with a shine as though only recently cleaned.

The tower must also have a way to refresh itself, either that or no dust exists in this magically created space...

She took another step forward, the sound of the heels of her boots against the stone echoing up in the vault of the chamber. The stair had no rail, and as she climbed the odd dimensions of the space continued to warp. Pausing, she looked over her shoulder, and her two companions had stopped at the third step, both moving toward the wall.

"The stair moves," Greysemmer called up to her.

No, but the magic does force itself against your mind making you believe so...

"You should wait," she replied.

They nodded, DireHammer running his hand over the stone wall and closing his eyes.

They won't be disoriented long, not working together...

Turning back, she continued her climb, the edge of the stair looming closer on her left until her feet brushed against the lip just before she made the first landing. Once there, she closed her eyes, took a deep breath, and then opened them again.

The world had corrected itself, and she moved away from the stair to another spiral flight of steps that led upward between the two lower curved entries. This one had walls on either side and their construction should have breached the exterior wall of the tower but somehow just kept going upward without incident.

She climbed again, up and up, each full revolution marked with an azure crystal set in the stones of the wall.

When her legs started to burn from the exertion, she paused and looked upward. The stair went on seemingly forever, the blue crystals illuminating the shaft drifting into a haze above.

It doesn't end...

She sat for a moment, leaning her back against the cool stone of the wall and watched below her. There was still no sign of the others, and she relaxed as her skin tingled with the *Afterglow* she'd received from the opening of the door.

If space is warped on the interior, then perhaps that too is a kind of foil to those who do not belong...

Opening her eyes, she looked up and down once more before finally settling on the crystal closest to her.

What is your purpose then, other than shaded illumination?

Standing, she moved the crystal and brushed her hand over its surface. There was momentary exchange of power and the crystal began to pulse, as did all those above and below.

You have a purpose don't you?

A vision of the airship tower of Mahe suddenly came to mind, and the elevator that she'd taken to the top.

Could it be?

She reached out again and pressed her palm against the pulsing crystal, then whispered, "Bedchamber."

There was a sudden shift, and some of the magic within her was drawn forth as the stairs around her bent and distorted until the crystal disappeared and an opening lay before her. She stepped through without pause, her head swimming, as she entered the pitch black.

Her boots struck stone, but she couldn't see, the darkness all enveloping.

You are in the house of a Wizard, and you have power, so you need to think as they would...

"Light," she called into the darkness.

The sound of stone sliding against stone echoed around her until four thin shafts of light split the dark. Each one grew steadily as golden light streamed into a large circular chamber and the smell of fresh air scented with honey blew around her.

Incredible...

Around her the sleeping chamber of Iquia lay as fresh as though slaves had cleaned it the morning before. It was sparsely decorated, only a single four poster bed, a small desk, and a wooden 'skeleton' for the hanging of a robe in the room. The floor was made of veined green tile, swirling patterns of turquoise and yellow mixed into it to create the sense of moving waves. Three tapestries hung on the walls, all of them depicting scenes of times long past when the Enlightened had first opened their Shining Cities and come forth to begin restoring the realms to their former glory with seeding and the release of animals.

She walked to the windows, the smell on the breeze intoxicating. Placing her hands against the smooth stone frame, only golden sky was in view, and silvered clouds hung in the space beyond. No sun was visible, nor was there a horizon. Instead, the warm glow of the exterior went on forever, both up and down, as though the tower window was set into a world of infinite space.

Only a single anomaly lay in the golden airy sea, a shining ripple in the distance that shifted in her vision from the shafts of glowing towers to the emerald green of fields and forests.

The Isle of Saints, can it really be?

She watched the distant land a long time as it continued to shift into mountains, then a city of impossible size with silver sailed ships in a harbor of rippling air.

"Saint Shera, if you are there, know that I strive to be the keeper of your wisdom, and I thank you for watching over me," she whispered.

On the distant Isle there was a flare of light, as though a signal had been set out for passing ships from the shore and her breast warmed until a smile spread across her face.

"You can hear me..." she said, and the flare pulsed again.

She stood there watching the display until her legs ached and she finally broke contact, the peace in her heart like the tranquility of a sea after a storm.

How can the power of the Wizards, my people, have been so great?

Turning slowly, she looked back into the room until her eyes rested on the drawn curtains of the great bed.

"I know you are here, Iquia, I saw it in my vision..." she whispered.

She slowly moved to the bed until she stood before the thick fabric, her hand trembling slightly as she ran her fingers against it.

No, this is your tomb, and I will not disturb your eternal slumber...

Pulling away, she took a step toward the crystal set in the far wall before her eye caught the robe still hanging from the wooden frame. It was long, voluminous, and made of grey silk trimmed in gold thread that created intricate runes over much of the surface.

She approached the robe, and let her hand run against it as her *Afterglow* was again exchanged and she felt the hairs stand up on the back of her neck.

It is said that the Wizards were of three houses, the Snow, the Ash, and the Ebon, each wearing some type of clothing that dedicated them to their school before being trimmed in gold...

She lifted the sleeve and the fabric carried almost no weight against her palm. Holding it, she looked back at the bed, and then sighed.

"Would you mind?" she asked.

The room gave a silent reply, and the peace in her heart remained.

"No, I'd think not, especially if I carry the blood of our people."

Gingerly, she drew the robe off the hanger and tried to slip it onto her arm. Like a coiling stream of water, the fabric resisted when it touched the sleeve of her leather jacket and she finally pulled it away to hold it before her again.

"What is it?" she asked.

She tried again, but it wouldn't go past her sleeve once more. Looking back at the bed, then the window, Skylla paused a long moment before she rehung the robe and then drew off her jacket.

Placing it on the floor, she bit her lip and then continued to disrobe until all her clothing lay in a pile to her left.

"I hope this works," she said.

Taking the robe once more, she pulled it over her arm and it slid onto her like a second skin, the fabric silken and cool against her flesh. She drew it over her head, and then down over her body, the fabric pooling on the floor around her feet as it was far too long for her.

Perhaps a good tailor could work with this, but I don't think I'd be comfortable in it as I've grown too used to my old leathers...

As if on cue, the fabric slithered and shifted around her, the hem creating grey boots with golden buckles, the rest of it morphing into grey leather pants with gold stitches, grey leather jacket with gold fastenings and filigree at the collar, and beneath it a supple silk blouse of mustard gold that clung to her like a second skin.

Impossible...

She spun around several times trying to get a good look at the outfit until she finally noticed what was missing.

Bands...

The jacket stretched at her neck and wrists, the honey-silvered metal of oricalcum bands coming into existence there.

I don't believe it...

For a moment she stared at her wrists before she closed her eyes and felt the presence of the robe around her, the power in it, and her connection to the reservoir of *Afterglow* within each arcane stich.

How did the Samaya ever defeat us...

The thought suddenly brought her eyes open, and she quickly reached down and picked up her belt and dagger harness, attaching it to her waist and thigh as she shook her head.

Us? What am I becoming? Remember who you are, Skylla, and don't let the power take you...

Moving quickly to the wall, she prepared to press her hand against the crystal, but then drew it back, instead pressing it against the wall.

For a moment her world tilted, but she used the *Afterglow* and pushed back, her mind reaching into the stone until she gained some control over it.

I wish to see Greysemmer and DireHammer...

The wall shifted before her eyes, become a translucent thing, and beyond it she could see the Human and Kin at the foot of the stair, a dozen plated and armed guards around them.

"She's been up there a long time," DireHammer said.

Greysemmer shook his head, "Too long, and I fear I may have miscalculated by giving her access to the tower in the first place."

"It was a risk we had to take, the magic is failing, and without the tower... or without her, we cannot maintain the safety of this place," DireHammer replied.

"I know, but she is a half-breed, and her mind has been corrupted by her contact with the Samaya and the blood within her. She may not help us, and I'm afraid we will be forced to gain her power in a more unseemly way," Greysemmer said.

"She's been a slave her whole life. Changing bands from one master to another shouldn't be a difficult transition, and if she learns her place, she might even become a fine breeder for a stock of water-born," DireHammer replied.

Skylla drew her hand back with a hiss, the power from the robe mixing with the essence she'd gained from the connection with the door until her hair became wet and she felt a tangle of golden threads slither from the robe around her fingers like gloves.

Damn my heritage, and damn those who would use me for it!

Reaching out, she touched the crystal and took a calming breath.

The entry foyer...

With a shift of the light, the room faded and a startled group of Enlightened appeared before her.

Greysemmer fell back a step, and the guards brought their spears around to face her, the room growing deadly quiet.

"There is nothing in this tower for you," she said.

DireHammer looked up at Greysemmer, and the shock on the man's face slowly bled away to a smile.

"Then there was something for you, as I see you've changed your clothing," he replied.

"I have, and I'll be leaving along with my ship, as we've nothing more to discuss, although I leave the contents of the tower to you, if you can breach its defenses."

"Daughter of the Deep," DireHammer began, "Why would you leave your own people who are in such need of your help only to return to the captivity of the Samaya?"

She turned toward the Kin, her hands beginning to glow and the guards lowered their spears further.

"You would have me leave a tarnished cage for one of gold? I heard you both, and I understand what you think of me and your plans to use what I am."

The sparks of fire lit heavy in the chamber, and the bloom of heat forced her to shield her eyes. DireHammer didn't pause as he extended his palm toward her and the marble floor shattered as a tendril of stone burst forth to strike her in the chest.

She was cast backward, the shock of the blow lessoned by magical wards on the transformed robe and likely the reserve of the Kin as he didn't wish her dead, only incapacitated. That was his mistake.

Rolling, she came up on one knee just as the spearman leapt at her. Casting her palm in an arch, she imagined a crashing wave and the *Afterglow* flowed from her in crashing reflection of her will. The energy struck the guards in a bright flash, their bodies cast backward like leaves in the wind.

I feel it. The power is within me, and I have more control than I did in the duel with Ethran, so long as I don't breach the barrier and take more than I already have inside...

DireHammer struck again, this time with twin lances of stone, each pointed and deadly, but she was ready, her energy creating a shield that crumbled both shafts before they could reach her.

"She is powerful!" DireHammer cried.

"Seal the door!" Greysemmer shouted back.

The Kin nodded and turned his attention to the door as those guards who had recovered from her impact wave now came at her from all sides, swords and spears at the ready.

Conserve what you can. This power is not endless...

She drew two knives from their sheaths on her thigh and met the first spear, turning it upward and then slipping beneath to run her second over the guard's abdomen. His armor warded the blow, and his spear ignited with a cool blue flame that hissed in the air as he tried again to strike her as she passed.

She sidestepped, but another guard brought his sword forward and caught her in the shoulder. The blow was half-deflected by the robe's magic, but the force still spun her around into the waiting attack of a third guard.

Another spear, this one rippling with blue fire came at her left arm, and she took the tip along her bicep, the fire igniting her blood and her hand dropping one of her knives.

She screamed, and beyond the combat caught site of DireHammer raising earth into the arch of the door to block any escape.

Damn the reserves!

Ducking into a ball, she imagined another wave, this one circular like the ripple of a drop of water on the surface of a pond. In the vision she channeled the bulk of the *Afterglow* she felt within her and also latently stored with the fabric of the robe.

There was a flash, like the shock of a bomb upon impact, and then a burst of destructive force radiated out from her in all directions.

Bones shattered, weapons crumbled, and the half completed wall of the Kin was blasted out into the entry beyond the verge as smoking rubble.

For a moment, Skylla expected another blow to fall, but instead her hair dripped onto the mosaic at her feet and she looked up to see nothing but ruin around her.

CHAPTER TEN

KALEB

There comes a moment as a captain when you must realize your strength does not lie within the confines of your own body, but instead in the will of those who serve under you. The greatest leader is always the one who has the finest soldiers, and that designation is how I feel about those who serve with me.

The Sand-Tyger is not a ship. It is the sum of the parts who man it, and among them I've come to trust Skylla more than most. Now I must trust her again, trust that she learned from her experiences with Ethran and that what we've shared in the months since that fateful campaign are as real to her as they have been to me.

"A light! Well, more a flash, but still," Parish said.

Stoneham was at the young man's shoulder in an instant, and Kaleb stood and stretched.

"He's right, although I only caught the tail end, but it was definitely from the bottom of the tower," Stoneham said.

"Then that is our signal, and if not, it won't matter anyway as they've either gotten what they wanted or Skylla is loose, and either way we'll not see morning if we stay here," Kaleb replied.

Stoneham handed his pistol to Parish, saying, "Two rounds, and aim for the head."

Parish nodded, and Kaleb looked at Brett. The young man's face was ashen, and he held his satchel to his chest as he whispered words to Saint Siegfried.

"You aren't a knight, so Siegfried isn't bound to listen unless you take up arms and prove your worth to him," Stoneham said.

Brett tried to say something, but there was movement at the door and everyone went silent as Kaleb pulled back the hammer on his weapon.

A fleeting moment passed before the door opened and two guards moved inside with visors down and their spears tipped with blue fire. Behind them the Lowl stood, his hands cupped around a ball of flickering blue flame and his eyes aglow.

Damn the Saints!

Kaleb raised his pistol, adjusted his line from the oncoming guards to the Lowl behind them and fired a single round of honey-oricalcum. Runes of warding flared around the guards as the bullet sped past, but they were shattered by the anti-magic, just as those warding the Lowl crumbled until the shell pierced his brain and lodged deep within.

The bullet was a relic of the final war, a round designed by the last Samayan tome-mages and imparted with the power of cancelling magic. Kaleb had discovered four such bullets in the ruins of a Samayan base high in the mountains the previous year, and after this shot, only one more remained to him.

The Lowl crumpled to the flags, his fire-seed dissipating and Parish following up with two shots of his own. The passing of Kaleb's round had disrupted the abjuration magic on the guard's armor, and although the first round was deflected on one of the enemy's helmet, the second found purchase in his lower jaw.

Stoneham was on the wounded guard in an instant, tearing the spear away and then launching it at the back of the other guard charging Kaleb. The fiery tip bit deep between the second guard's shoulder blades and he tumbled forward with a strangled scream.

The first guard held his ruined face, but Stoneham ended him with a steel-tipped boot and then retrieved the extinguished spear from the body of the second, Parish taking a position at the door with his pistol at the ready.

"All clear," Parish said.

Outside, thunder boomed and the rain increased as sheets lashed through the open shutters.

"Let's move," Kaleb instructed.

Stoneham patted Parish on the shoulder and then moved past him, the two making their way out into the rain as Kaleb fingered the final Nul round before opening the cylinder on his pistol and replacing the spent casing with the fresh bullet.

"We'll be killed," Brett whispered.

Kaleb snapped the cylinder closed and turned to the archeologist, "Maybe, but we're not going to die without a fight. Are you with us?"

Brett was staring at the bodies slowly bleeding onto the floor, but blinked at the last words and looked up. At last, he nodded, and Kaleb turned away, moving to follow Parish and Stoneham, the sounds of Brett's footfalls close behind.

The rain was so heavy Kaleb could barely see five feet in front of him, and his small band kept close as they crossed the first bridge back toward the tower.

"No resistance," Stoneham shouted.

"Yeah, the rain will keep the fire-born inside I'd think, and the Aspara and Kin looked too few when we arrived to mount search parties," Kaleb replied.

Stoneham nodded, rain pouring off his jaw in a constant stream.

"Keep moving, we should pass between three buildings on this isle and then we'll make the bridge to the water tower," Kaleb said.

They moved on, the path slithering between three stone cottages, golden light leaking out into the night from closed shutters.

Just as they passed the third dwelling, a small shape appeared on the path and Parish raised his pistol only to be struck down by a hammer. Stoneham intercepted the enemy before a second strike could finish Parish, his spear coming into contact with the heavy-headed weapon with a crisp clang.

The quartermaster adjusted his stance and started to push the smaller enemy back, but the ground undulated beneath his feet, and he was cast into the air before landing awkwardly on his back.

Kaleb thumbed the cylinder forward as single revolution to clear the remaining Null round, and then fired a standard bullet. Runes sprang to life on the smaller enemy illuminating the broad shoulders and bat-ears of a Kin.

Firing a second round, the Kin let out a guttural challenge and charged, his body shifting and growing with each step until he was more charging lizardman than stout humanoid. After the fourth round the Kin was within ten feet, his defensive matrix glowing crimson and his hammer raised.

Snapping his fifth round off, Kaleb saw the matrix shatter, but it was too late, the hammer ready to end him until a blaze of phosphorescent light burst into existence behind his left shoulder.

The enraged Kin screeched, his blow faltering as he ground to a halt and shielded his small black eyes. Behind the Enlightened, Stoneham rose up, the light showing blood coming from the man's lip and left eye, but he raised his spear and plunged it down into the back of the Kin with all his might.

Kaleb opened the cylinder, replaced a spent round, and then snapped it closed as the Kin turned toward Stoneham with his head downturned to shield it from the light.

Again the hammer raised, but Kaleb fired his fresh round into the back of the Kin's skull and it slowed, hammer dropping from numb fingers until it toppled over onto the path.

Behind Kaleb the light flickered, and he turned to see Brett with a flare held out in a trembling hand.

"The texts said Kin were dayblind. That was why they wore masks. Bright light hurt their eyes," he said.

Kaleb nodded, adding, "Well done."

Snapping open his cylinder once more, he expelled five casings. The sixth was still in place as he'd avoided using the Null. He then replaced the spent ones with fresh ones from his belt. Stoneham moved up the path and looked over at the fallen Parish, finally getting the young man to his feet although only with a great deal of support.

"Broken ribs I'd think," Stoneham said.

Parish's head hung low, one arm over Stoneham's shoulder, but in the other he still clutched the small caliber revolver.

"Can you go on?" Kaleb asked.

"Yes sir," Parish wheezed.

Kaleb turned back to Brett, "Better douse that, or leave it."

Brett tossed the flare next to the Kin's body, and the party moved on over the bridge to the water tower. Finally they came into view amid the haze of the midnight storm.

Twin flashes of lighting danced amid the din of rushing water as the party moved across the bridge toward the tower. Reaching into his coat, Kaleb removed the field glasses and raised them to his eyes. Darkness reigned across the bridge, but he could make out the silhouette of two red and one blue persons lurking on the far side.

"We've got two fire-born and an air-born," he said.

Stoneham paused, and Kaleb thumbed the cylinder in his pistol until the Nul round was aligned with the hammer.

Another flash of light lit the tower, but this time from below instead of the sky. The party ducked down along the span as Kaleb raised the glasses once more.

The magically blessed binoculars searched further toward the tower. Another dull brown silhouette was fading quickly from view and a deep green one moved toward the bridge.

"Skylla! She's on her way," he said.

Stoneham nodded, and Parish wheezed something unintelligible.

"Brett, you take Parish. Stoneham, keep that spear ready," Kaleb ordered.

Parish was transferred, and inside the vision provided by the goggles Kaleb watched Skylla approach the three enemy Enlightened on the far side of the bridge, each turning to move toward her.

"That's our cue. Let's move," he ordered.

The party slipped across the far side of the bridge, and Kaleb advanced the cylinder again to a normal bullet before an airburst turned the rain sideways and blew plants back against the ground. Brett and Parish tumbled back, and Kaleb lost his hat, but for a moment he made out an Aspara floating five feet off the ground as he summoned a vortex of wind about him.

Raising his pistol, he fired once, twice, and a third time, the enemy's elemental defensive matrix flaring with white runes and twin eruptions' blue flame coming into existence below the Aspara as it turned the rain away from the field in a kind of dome.

He wards the water from the fire-born below…

Balls of green-blue flame rocketed up toward the bridge, and Kaleb dove to the side as one impacted the stone and wood frame in a steaming explosion that sent bits of debris in every direction.

Stoneham was already on the move, his spear held over his shoulder in a launch-ready position.

You'll never penetrate that defense…

As the words rattled in his mind, he saw another flare, this one golden, break out of the far side of the windy globe. It took the form of a Gander's Hawk, the small sea predator shooting up and out of the rain to pierce the Asparan matrix before it pulled its wings close and turned into a golden arrow.

The head of the golden weapon struck the Aspara in the breast, and Kaleb tumbled to the ground as the rain resumed unabated with the wind dropping with him. The flames of the fire-born were extinguished with a high pitched hiss, and Kaleb fired two more rounds into one of the targets before he lost sight of it.

The fire-born's matrix failed, and the head of a spear breached it a moment later as the Enlightened screamed a keening wail and then went down.

"Brett, you good?" Kaleb asked.

The archeologist struggled to get Parish back to his feet but nodded an affirmative. Kaleb turned back and brought the glasses to his eyes. The final fire-born was on the move, his essence leaving a trail of crimson across the island to the far side and another bridge there.

"We're clear for the moment," he said.

Brett brought Parish forward, and the three of them quickly found Stoneham removing his spear from the chest of a man no larger than a ten-year old boy. He was perfectly proportioned, and had a wild mop of blue hair atop his cherub face with eyes still burning like the stoked coals of a dying fire.

"An Eldaryn," Brett whispered.

"Whatever he was, it's no more a concern of ours," Stoneham said.

From the far side of the windblown clearing, Skylla appeared. She was rain-soaked and her right arm bled down to her fingers. Kaleb holstered his pistol and raced to her before she half-collapsed against him.

"What happened?" he asked.

She was shaking, the dark circles around her eyes a mark of her overuse of magic and the toll it took on her body.

"They tried to stop me..." she whispered.

Kaleb nodded, brushed her violet hair back from her eyes and then picked her up. She was incredibly light, and he watched as her clothes repelled the water like a sheet of tin, the colors and texture not the same as they had been hours before.

"Stoneham!" Kaleb yelled.

The quartermaster was at his side in an instant.

"Take the point and get us back to the ship," Kaleb instructed.

Stoneham nodded, adjusted his grip on the spear, and then moved off toward another bridge. Kaleb followed, Skylla resting her head against his shoulder as he smelled the salty tang of the sea.

CHAPTER ELEVEN

SKYLLA

I don't like to be saved, unless, that is, I like to be saved. I know that probably makes no sense, but often makes sense to the heart rarely has a place in a firm grasp of reality...

Skylla could hear Kaleb's heart beating rapidly in his chest, smell his musky and tobacco scent, and feel the tremors of each fall of his boots as he moved through the storm. She closed her eyes, drifted until she could see the *Sand-Tyger* sitting in the port of Mahe as the crew was entertained by Mya dancing for them on the starboard pontoon.

She smiled at the vision, and she wanted to be there, clapping along with the rest, but instead the rain continued to fall in the dark and a shout woke her suddenly from the delirium.

"Get the ship ready!" Stoneham yelled.

Raising her head form Kaleb's chest, she caught sight of the *Gypsy Sky* as the ship swung wildly in its berth. Lights twinkled in the windows along the belly, and Lance was standing next to a lantern at the entry plank in a slicker and with a rifle at the ready.

"Tell Charles to get the ship ready to move!" Stoneham shouted again.

"It's raining!" Lance yelled back.

"Just do it!" Stoneham growled.

Lance disappeared up the plank and Skylla looked up at Kaleb as he struggled through the rain toward the waiting craft.

"You lost your hat," she said.

He looked down, somehow a smile finding his lips.

"Better it than you," he replied.

She laughed, then bit her lip as pain shot up her arm. Kaleb kept moving and by the time he'd made the shaky assent to the *Gypsy's* superstructure Doc Rose was already waiting.

Kaleb lowered her down gently and she found her footing, swaying a moment before putting her good arm on an interior rail and stood on her own.

"What happened?" Rose asked.

"There was an issue about Skylla staying, and I don't think it's been fully resolved yet," Kaleb said.

Rose nodded, opened his bag and then waived for Brett to rest Parish against an interior wall. Outside, Stoneham fired a rifle taken from Lance when he'd gone to help launch the ship, and Kaleb reloaded his pistol.

Skylla moved toward the entry, but Rose held her, bandages in his hand.

"Let them deal with it a moment, won't you?" he asked.

She looked from Rose to Kaleb, then back, nodding. More fire proceeded, and the ship lurched as the engines were ignited.

"The ship shouldn't be flying in this, the rains making it too heavy to maintain altitude, especially after the gas we vented," Brett said.

"Charles knows what he's doing," Skylla replied.

"Or he's got no other choice," Rose said.

The doctor dabbed the wound on her arm with alcohol and then began wrapping it, saying, "This is a field dressing. You'll need stitches at the very least once we've more time."

"Stoneham, get back here!" Kaleb yelled.

Stoneham fell back inside the threshold, and Kaleb fired three shots before the ship lurched and then fell away from the dock with the plank tumbling out into the night sky.

"Nice shot," Stoneham smiled.

"Thanks," Kaleb said, forcing the door closed.

The ship pitched again, and everyone held onto something as they continued to descend.

"What's happening?" Stoneham asked.

"We're not ready to fly, especially under these weather conditions," Kaleb said.

When the ship righted itself, rain still hammering the windows, Kaleb moved up the deck toward the bridge. Skylla followed after him, Doc Rose having gone to attend to Parish who was struggling to breathe.

"If we've lost too much gas…" she trailed off.

Kaleb nodded, "I know, but we couldn't stay there."

"Captain," Stoneham called, "Something is happening above us!"

Skylla exchanged a look at Kaleb and then they both went to the nearest window and looked up. Above them the dark shape of the island still hung in the storm, and light blazed in two open caves beneath one of the islands.

"Wonderful. They have airships," Kaleb said.

"If I can get to an opening," she began.

Kaleb cut her off, his eyes hard and a hand going out to grip her by the shoulder.

"No, you've done enough, and there are no miracles in the sky to save you this time," he said.

"But,"

He shook his head.

"I won't lose you that way, not while we have other choices."

"What other choices?" she asked.

"Charles is a good captain or you wouldn't have picked him. Let's see what he thinks about this."

She nodded, her stomach churning.

Saint Shera, this man is my world, don't take him from me yet…

Together, they continued forward toward the bridge.

"Nothing yet, Captain," Paul said from the navigator's node above their heads.

Charles was spinning dials and engaging levers as Skylla and Kaleb came onto the bridge, his face pale and his clothes covered in grease.

"Can we help?" Kaleb asked.

Charles didn't look up. "Do you have any spare lift gas on you?"

Kaleb didn't answer, instead moving to a front window and taking another look at the island above, asking, "How long do we have?"

"A couple of hours in good weather, half that if the rain continues," Charles replied.

"It won't matter if the Enlightened launch something to come after us," Skylla said.

Charles turned, looked at her arm, then moved his gaze to another panel of gauges, saying, "Well, then we'll have to use our reserves."

"Reserves?" Kaleb and Skylla asked at the same time.

"Better buckle yourselves in," he said.

Flipping two switches, Charles moved back to his captain's chair and then leaned into a conical horn to his right.

"Attention, this is the captain. Buckle yourselves in as we are about to use the booster rocket," he said.

"Those were only experimental," Kaleb said.

Charles turned to him and nodded, "True, and it's good you know your naval history, but what the governments didn't want, they threw out, and scavengers got the best pickings. Oh, and did I mention I'm a great scavenger?"

"But they caused dozens of ships to crash!" Kaleb replied.

"We're going to crash anyway," Charles said.

Skylla grabbed Kaleb's arm and pulled him toward a set of flip-down seats at the back wall of the bridge, shoulder straps accompanying each.

"He knows what he's doing," she said.

"He'd better," Kaleb replied.

They buckled in, and she hissed once as the strap contacted her wound, but when she was done, Charles called up to Paul.

"Release the ballast and vent the water veins," he ordered.

Paul reached out and moved several levers as the sound of gears overshadowed the pounding rain. The *Gypsy* lurched again, this time the nose pointing up just as two ships slipped from the island above with light streaming from their sides.

"Bring us due east," Charles said.

Paul complied and the nose of the ship turned away from the enemy craft as Charles reached to his right and grabbed an ivory-handled lever there.

"Ready?" he asked.

Before anyone could answer, he threw the lever and the whine of a cycling booster roared up from somewhere deep in the ship. An instant later, everyone was thrown back in their seats. The initial thrust faded quickly, and the thousand screaming protests from the ships superstructure calmed to a thrumming din as vibrations continued to shake the frame in a constant shimmy.

"Well, at least we didn't blow up," Charles said.

"There's that," Kaleb replied.

"You're drifting, keep her due east, Mr. Paul." Charles ordered.

"It's like wrestling a greased pig, Captain, she's insistent on going where the storm takes her," Paul replied.

Charles nodded, and then unstrapped himself from his chair before going to the window to get a look behind them.

"I'd say the storm will continue to bring us down, but at least the pursuit has fallen off," he said.

"How many miles can we get?" Kaleb asked.

"Well into the Madras on a full burn, but we'll likely run directly into a mountainside before that," Charles replied.

"Fantastic," Kaleb said, unbuckling as well.

"Captain?" Skylla asked.

"I'm going to check on Parish and see if we've got any other tricks up our sleeves," he said.

He left without another word and she turned back to Charles who was leaning against a gauge panel and smiling at her.

"You're bleeding," he said.

She looked down at her arm, the bandage stained with crimson and a single channel of blood going down her forearm to the bracer at her wrist.

"I'll live," she said.

"I have no doubt of that, but I have to wonder if what happened back there will let the rest of us be so lucky."

"Maybe it just bought us some time, but without the stop we'd have been grounded before the storm even hit, so there's that," she replied.

"When you hired me, I knew there was something different about you, but you being an Enlightened wasn't in my range of consideration," he said.

"Would it have mattered?"

"Maybe," he paused, "Maybe I'd have taken the job a bit faster."

"Really, and why is that?"

He shrugged, "Because in this life, you don't get to see a dying race very often, and maybe I wanted to tell my grandkids about it."

"Spoken like a true adventurer, both inspiring and comically antiseptic," she replied.

"Antiseptic?" he asked.

"Yes, like most Samaya, you somehow consider your own responsibility for what is happening in the world a non-factor, as though you are clear of blame because you don't run a country."

"That's not really fair," he began.

She undid her buckles, cutting him off, "Fair is being compassionate enough to understand that extinction isn't an answer or an anecdote, but something you have a responsibility to see doesn't happen."

Before he could go any further, she left the bridge, her legs trembling and the ache in her arm pulsing with each step.

She met Doc Rose halfway to her quarters, and he had his bag with him and a dozen wrinkles between his eyes.

"Kaleb sent me to find you," he offered.

A dull laugh escaped her lips, "Of course he did."

Rose adjusted his glasses, "Meaning?"

"Meaning there is nothing careless about the captain, and that is why I'm with him," she replied.

"That is why we are all with him," Rose said.

"No, not all," she replied as she looked further down the hall to the room of Vivian Malett.

Nodding, Rose took her hand and led her into her room. She complied, the thrum of the ship making her tired, or perhaps the loss of blood, but she didn't complain when Rose gave her a flask of strong spirits, the man making small talk as he prepared to stitch her wound.

CHAPTER TWELVE

KALEB

I know I've said this before, and I'll say it again. The hardest part of being a leader is knowing that you must sacrifice your subordinates for the good of the whole. I'm not yet prepared to do this, but nonetheless it is something I face in the imminent future.

Now I must keep the crew together and find a way to bring this mission home because I cannot be the cause of my children's orphaning, as both their parents lives are now in dire jeopardy...

Kaleb stood over Parish as he lay in his bed, bandages wrapped around his chest and his breathing ragged.

I shouldn't have brought him...

"Captain?" Parish asked, opening his eyes.

"How are you doing, Mr. Parish?"

He tried to sit up, hissed, and then lay back down. "Good, Sir. Doc Rose says I'll be up and around in no time."

"That's a good thing, as I'm sure we'll need you."

Parish smiled.

"Is the ship safe?" he asked.

Kaleb nodded, "Yes, but I've some other stuff that needs dealing with on that end. I wanted to make sure you were doing well."

"Ship shape," the young man replied.

"Good, than get some rest."

"Yes, sir."

Moving from the room, he headed further aft, the words of Doc Rose ringing in his ears.

'His insides are broken, and I can't stop the bleeding without surgery'...

He ran a hand through his hair.

That is going to be a problem, but right now we might all be dead before he goes to meet his patron saint...

Taking a side passage, he moved to the crystal room, Tolbert busily working on an alignment as the runes on his scarf glowed a warm gold.

"How goes it, Mr. Tolbert?" he asked.

The junior mage-tech looked up, his goggles catching the light of the tech crystal with an eerie blue glow.

"She's holding, Captain, and Charles's rocket is somehow managing to draw power without fully compromising the other engines."

"He must be a good tech himself," Kaleb offered.

"Indeed, and the draft matrix is astonishing, assuming he also designed it."

"Then we should count ourselves lucky."

Tolbert nodded, ran his hand over a gauge and whispered an unintelligible word. The gauge came to life, and the rune scarf flared again as steam blew from several valves above his head.

"Charles says we'll never get enough altitude to cross the mountains," Kaleb said.

Tolbert turned around, tapped a couple of other gauges and nodded, "Looks that way. He's got a nice inner tank reserve of Delta X, which is keeping us up now, but the standard lift tanks are nearly empty."

"Any ideas?" he asked.

Tolbert shook his head, "I can't create gas, at least the kind that would help, and although I can up the engines output, that will just drive us downward without the lift compensation."

"Noted. Just keep us flying, I'll come up with something."

With a half-salute, Tolbert went back to work and Kaleb left the din of the power room until he could lean his back against the cool wood of a hallway wall and close his eyes.

If we've got no other choice, I'll have to go to Skylla...

"Bad news?"

He didn't open his eyes, instead shaking his head as he heard Vivian draw closer, her booted heels clicking on the planks of the hall's teak floor.

"There is a problem with the lift gas," he said.

"Can you fix it?"

"Doesn't look that way."

He smelled her draw close, easing in next to him on the wall until her shoulder rested against his upper arm.

"Does stuff like this happen very often in your adventures?"

"Pretty much."

"And you always make it out unscathed?"

"Not unscathed. There is always a cost."

"I heard one of your crew was seriously injured."

"Parish. He's not going to make it without surgery."

"I'm sorry."

"Me too. He's a sharp kid."

"Is there anything I can do?"

"If you have some spare lift gas up yours skirt, I'd like to know about it."

"What makes you think I have on a skirt?"

He kept his eyes closed and resisted the urge to look.

"You've always got on a skirt."

"And you like women in pants, is that it?"

He sighed, saying, "I'm not having this discussion."

There was a protracted pause; then she pushed away from him and the sound of her footfalls drifted up the hall.

"I think the girl in pants is tough enough to do what you need her to," Vivian called over her shoulder.

A door closed quickly afterward and he sighed before opening his eyes.

We can certainly hope so…

The storm broke before the sun came up, the steel-grey clouds still thick around the ship as it dropped further down into the glow of the dawn. From the bridge, Kaleb watched as mountains were silhouetted below, the white snows along their ridges showing winter's grip still lingered in the high country of inner Aflyr.

Further out, higher peaks loomed, and he bit his lower lip as he contemplated them.

"We won't be able to pass them. The cold air and condensation will ice us and we'll be grounded in less than an hour," Charles offered.

"Can we turn back?"

"I could gut the rocket and we could try, but we'd be moving directly into the teeth of the pursuit, because Paul reported seeing lights in the distance all through the storm last night."

"Then we have to find a way through."

"But I can't navigate that, not with the ice and the speed we've got going."

Kaleb pushed away from the glass and moved toward the exit, calling over his shoulder when he breached the door, "Just keep us going forward."

He entered the hall, Stoneham looking out one window with Greylin next to him. They didn't speak, and he didn't either. Instead, he moved past them to Skylla's room. He was about to knock when Doc Rose opened the door. Kaleb's fist paused in the air.

"She's still asleep," Rose said.

"Then I'll have to wake her," he replied.

"No, I can't let you…"

"Kaleb?" Skylla called from the interior.

Rose's face grew red, but he backed away, his voice hissing a warning as Kaleb passed him, "Don't burden her."

The doctor closed the door, and Kaleb moved to where Skylla now sat, her skin pale and her eyes dark.

"You look better than Parish," he said.

"How is he?"

"Not good, but none of us are out of mortal danger at the moment."

"The ship?"

"We can't get over the mountains, and the Enlightened are still in pursuit."

She nodded, threw off her covers and slipped her legs over the edge of the cot. She wore a sleeveless grey nightgown, trimmed with golden thread, and he was about to look for her clothes when he noted she had no bands around her neck and wrists.

"What happened to your bands?" he asked.

She looked down absently and then closed her eyes. The nightgown crawled over her like a living thing and Kaleb took a step back as his hand went to his pistol. The fabric shifted, took on greater volume, and in moments she was dressed in her familiar boots, pants, and jacket, all now grey and trimmed in gold, complete with the oricalcum bands at her wrists and neck.

"How?" he asked.

"Greysemmer had a Kin remove my bands when I took in the Afterglow stores of the water tower. When I was inside, I found the robes of a long dead Wizard, and it seems they can mimic any outfit I desire," she replied.

Anything you desire?

He nodded, coughed and then asked, "Do you still have power?"

"A little, and the robes draw some from me as well to store it as I need."

"Can you create more gas?" he asked.

She shook her head, "No, I don't have that kind of control, but I do think I can do something," she answered.

"Skylla, I know this is…"

Placing a finger to his lips, she stopped him. "I know the risks of who I am, and you didn't ask. I'm doing this on my own, so you just promise to be there to catch me when I collapse."

He nodded, and she gave him a sad smile.

"But you'll owe me," she added.

Pushing past him, she got halfway to the door before he grabbed her good arm, pulled her back around and kissed her. She resisted only a moment, then fell fully against him as she put her arms around his neck and the smell of the ocean filled the room.

Her hair dripped down onto his hands at the small of her back and he tasted salt, but he didn't let go until he was forced to draw a deep breath. She was looking up at him, her eyes like polished emeralds.

I've never seen you so foreign and so beautiful…

"What was that?" she asked.

"I wanted to be sure you knew what you'd be missing if this killed you," he said, a smile crossing his lips.

She laughed, "Well, Captain, I think you made your point."

CHAPTER THIRTEEN

SKYLLA

Now is the time to discover the truth of the power that is within me, assuming that truth doesn't kill me first...

Kaleb descended the ladder to one of rear landing observation nodes, and she followed using her injured arm gingerly. Rose had given her a dose of painkiller which made her feel both numb and exhilarated at the same time.

Before she hit the lander's station deck, Kaleb grabbed her around the waist and helped her down gently. She smiled and turned to look over her shoulder at him in the confined space.

"You really can't keep your hands off me today," she said.

"Well, it is nice to get some private time with you. Too bad those cliffs wouldn't allow more of it," he replied.

She followed his line of vision to the oncoming mountains, now so close she could make out the intricacies of the sediment in the rocks and the mists of snow being blown about along the ridges.

"Charles's kept us clear so far, but I'd say it's only a matter of minutes now as we continue to drop," Kaleb said.

As if on cue, Charles's voice came over a speaker, "Attention all crew! Prepare for a crash landing."

Ahead, a series of jagged peaks blocked out the horizon, each one like a sabre pointed up to open the *Gypsy's* exposed belly.

"Can you do anything?" Kaleb asked.

She nodded, closed her eyes and took a deep breath.

Concentrate and make contact with the Afterglow…

The robe prickled her skin, and she could feel Afterglow residue there. It wasn't much, but she drew it into her body like a child working a soda-shop straw to get the last of an ice-milk drink from the bottom of a tall glass.

When the final essence was within her, she found the memory of the time when her and Ethran walked along the cliffs beneath the ruined Samaya city when he'd called the sky whales to her hand. They were huge creatures, their backs covered with gas pockets that smugglers and poachers still harvested because of the lift it could provide an airship.

Once the picture was there, she opened her eyes and stretched her palms out as she stared through the glass. A shimmer appeared in the sky beneath the *Gypsy*, and slowly she released her Afterglow as she shaped a representation of the whale she'd touched half a year before.

The glow grew and grew, and her power reserves dwindled as she shaped and wrought the energy into a facsimile of the creature she'd met.

She could feel water streaming down her back, and see the threads of Afterglow pass through the glass into the creature like a thousand spider spinners working as one.

The vision wasn't complete as she felt that last ebb of her magic but she held it, secured a tether, and then let out a shuddering breath.

Don't spend it all, and don't open yourself like you did in the battle with Ethran…

What hovered beneath the *Gypsy* wasn't exactly an air whale, but it was close enough, and she pushed her will against her creation bringing it up and into contact with the bulk of the ship above.

The *Gypsy* shuddered at the impact, and she leaned forward, her arms trembling and the cold of the high altitude forming crystals on the back of her wet hands. Behind her, Kaleb pulled off his coat and brought it over her shoulders, his scent and the warm of the stored body heat giving her some strength.

Willing the glowing creature up again, she felt the strain in her shoulders, her back and down her legs, but she continued to push.

The creation moved with her, large wings flapping down as it pushed up, the nose of the *Gypsy* going with it as the horizontal plane shifted slightly.

"You're doing it," Kaleb whispered.

Yes, but Saint Shera help me to have the strength to continue…

Pushing hard again, she drew more will from her mind, and the whale beat even harder at the air, it's back pressing against the ship as they continued to climb.

Before them the jagged cliffs drew closer, each one like a city tower, but the Afterglow engines buzzed and the guide wings of the ship turned as they sped past the first of the mountain's upturned teeth.

She pressed again, and the ship climbed further, more of the mountain passing beneath. But there were still three towers ahead that could not be overcome at their current altitude.

Raising both her hands, she bit her lip and let the Kaleb's coat fall away, mist flowing from her nose in a great exhale as the whale fought against gravity and the weight of the craft above it.

Her legs shook, and Kaleb was there, his arms wrapping around her waist again, this time from behind as he held her. His strength reinforced her will, and she let out a scream as she exerted all her muscles in a final strain.

The whale echoed her cry with one of its own, the strange sound rising above the din of the engines and rocket to reverberate in the mountains below. Cascades of snow broke loose from ancient rocks and slid downward into a haze of white.

Still, the ship climbed again, and the once deadly towers fell away from their line of sight as the grey morning was replaced with a sun-painted blue sky and rippled white clouds beyond the ranges upper heights.

"The sea," Kaleb whispered.

She looked out beyond her creation, and the mountains stretched east for miles, then broke into green that lay like a blanket until giving way to the azure waters of the Madras, great inner sea of the Old Kingdoms.

Giving one last push with her mind, the whale moved them up further until her head swam and she faltered. In her collapse, she released the Afterglow and the whale burst asunder like a firework of twinkling embers that fell away into the sky below.

Kaleb kept her upright, and she could feel the crispness of the frost on her skin and robes as he called into a cone used by the landing operator.

"We need some help in the landing cone!"

She shivered, and he rubbed her shoulders, her hair cracking with ice as he moved it and rewrapped her in his jacket.

"I'll live," she smiled weakly.

"Unless you freeze first," he replied.

She shook her head, "Water, even frozen, cannot claim me."

He furrowed a brow, and she felt strange as though the words themselves were not hers to speak.

Lance was the first to slide down the ladder, and she let Kaleb deal with the newcomer, her eyes glazing over as she stoked the last wisp of Afterglow in her chest, the ember keeping her water-spark alive.

CHAPTER FOURTEEN

KALEB

She always finds a way, and that is just one of many reasons I've fallen in love with her. It is a road that I see no resolution on, no happy ending, and yet I would take it willingly if it meant walking with her into some unknown oblivion.

Perhaps that is foolish, but love is inherently so, wouldn't you say? Is this why you watch, to see how two people from different worlds will collide when everyone else seems to want to rip them apart? Am I overdramatic? Conspiracies don't become a strong man, and I can't blame fate or the world for what has happened here, but I still believe there is a hand working I cannot discern.

Whatever the case, I move forward with the knowledge that although another woman claims my legal adherence, Skylla is the one who will forever have my heart.

Kaleb stood with Charles, both men looking over a map spread across a drop-down table on the bridge. Above, Paul worked to steer the *Gypsy* as Charles called out marks.

Taking a compass, Kaleb walked it over the map's surface between a pin that represented the ship and the sea around it. He checked again and again, but the final point always ended in the same place, three hundred miles off the coast of what had once been the Kuhjan Empire.

"There is nothing there," Kaleb stated for the fourth time.

"But your map indicates the *SkyGlaive* is at that point," Charles replied.

Kaleb nodded, took out his map, and then rechecked the longitude and latitude.

"Perhaps it is a base, something not on the map," Charles offered.

"Maybe, but if this map is wrong, or we miss it, then the Madras will swallow us up as I'm afraid Skylla can't make another miracle," Kaleb replied.

From the entry, Brett appeared, and Kaleb waved him in. The young man came forward and adjusted his glasses as he looked down at the map.

"What's this?" he asked.

"A map of the Madras," Charles replied.

Brett looked it over, made several ticking sounds with his tongue and then shook his head. "Well, that may be, but it isn't one of the old world maps."

Kaleb looked up, "Meaning?"

Reaching into his pack, Brett pulled out a book and flipped through it until he came to a two-page spread that roughly depicted the map on Charles's navigation table. Placing it on the surface, he adjusted it so that the two captains could have a good vantage.

"You see, your map is a survey, and it looks like those who made it kept to the shoreline which makes a viable image of the Madras, but it doesn't let you see what is out in the water," Brett said.

Kaleb looked down and compared the two. On Brett's map there were more than a dozen islands shown, two of which were large, and one of those fell directly into the coordinates of the *SkyGlaive*.

"There," Kaleb pointed at the island in question.

Charles nodded and placed a pin in the map on the table marking where the island would be located.

Brett was shaking his head. "What is that?"

"The location of the *SkyGlaive*," Kaleb answered.

"You're saying it is on that island?"

"Yes."

Brett pushed his glasses back into place once more and pulled the book back as he flipped several pages.

"What is it?" Kaleb asked.

"Yanoan," Brett replied.

"Who?" Kaleb and Charles asked in unison.

Brett shook his head, "It's not a who, it's a place, the realm of the Farians."

"More Enlightened, and air-touched, but they've been destroyed by all accounts," Charles said.

"Perhaps, but in my research it was said that the Farians were the most advanced of the Enlightened, a people that reflected the lifespan of the immortal Aspara but the driving fire of Human creation," Brett said.

"So Air and Fire," Kaleb said.

"Exactly! The Yanoan were the technological masters of the Enlightened, and they were the first to develop modern airships, mechanized walkers, and high capacity firearms," Brett continued.

"Then why would the *SkyGlaive* be on their island?" Charles asked.

Kaleb shrugged, "I don't know, but the better question is, 'Will we make it there?'"

Charles took the book from Brett, flipped back to the map and then compared it to his. After a moment of furrowed brow, he sighed, saying, "It will be close."

"Then at least we've got a shot," Kaleb said.

"But, Captain," Brett began, "If we've recently seen Enlightened in the sky above eastern Aflyr, and the Madras is even more remote, wouldn't it be likely..."

"That there are Enlightened on Yanoan, probably, but at this point we don't have much choice in the matter," Kaleb finished.

Brett nodded, his face pale, and Charles shouted a course correction to Paul above in the navigation bubble.

The rocket had cut out just after they'd reached the deep shelf of Madras, and by late afternoon the sea dominated everything to the horizon.

Kaleb watched the water from the bridge, Charles asleep in his command chair and Paul reading a book in the navigator's station above.

It's not how I'd run a ship, but here I'm just a passenger and I've got to remember that...

Doc Rose entered the bridge and Charles stirred but didn't wake, the older man moving quietly past the captain until he stood next to Kaleb.

"The sea is all about," Rose said.

"Yes, it's a race against time now."

Rose drew off his glasses and wiped the lenses. Kaleb kept his eyes on the waves, whitecaps now visible from their dwindling elevation.

"I've given Parish a sleep serum, but his breathing is growing more labored," Rose said.

"Then we all run short on time," Kaleb replied.

"If we manage a landing, I'll operate, but the conditions will still be far from ideal."

Kaleb nodded, "Is there anything I can do?"

"No, my friend, just give a prayer to Saint Erik for some luck that I find the inner wound and can deal with it before he bleeds out," Rose said.

"With the blood already filling his abdomen, the odds aren't good," Kaleb said.

"True, but I see no other choice, and a transfusion isn't possible."

A pod of dolphins surfaced to the west and Kaleb eyed them, their play somehow bringing him comfort.

"What about a Salvation Pack?" Kaleb asked.

Rose shook his head, "If we had one, don't you think I'd know about it?"

"Of course, but if the *SkyGlaive* exists, there's a chance it still carries munitions and supplies not seen in the Realms since the final days of the war," Kaleb said.

"Those packs have done more miracles than the Saints, Kaleb, but do you really believe it's possible the ship would have one?"

"Anything is possible where the *Glaive* is concerned."

"Then what would you have me do?" Rose asked.

"Keep Parish resting, and alive, as long as you can, but don't open him up."

"If you don't find the ship, or if it doesn't have a pack, you've relegated him to death without a chance," Rose said.

"And how much chance would your surgery provide?" Kaleb asked.

Rose sighed but didn't answer.

"Then leave the boy closed, and let me worry about miracles," Kaleb said.

There was a protracted pause, both men looking at the pod of dolphins for some time before Rose spoke again.

"Skylla is recovering. After a few hours of sleep, I checked her wound and it was only a pink scar, whatever magic she now holds, or by some power in her strange new clothing, the healing properties are incredible."

"Many were the tales of the Enlightened taking grievous wounds only to be seen fresh on the field of battle the next day," Kaleb said.

"Then the tales must hold more truth than I'd have given them credit, but I was just a hospitaler when the war ended, so I couldn't have spoken to such claims until now as I'd no experience on the front."

"Perhaps it's because she's a Wizard," Kaleb offered.

"Half-Wizard," Rose corrected.

"Half-Wizard then, but whatever the case, her race should have died out half a century ago, as they were the fewest in number of any Enlightened by the start of the war, and certainly the most vigorously hunted during it."

"Such power can be both a blessing and a curse," Rose offered.

"As is the case in how she deals with the use of her magic. Each time it seemingly brings her to the brink of death."

Rose shook his head, "True, but she's just learning to use the power, and the more she does so, the stronger she'll become and I'd think the better able to deal with the burden of using it."

"Makes sense, much like any skill one has to learn fresh," Kaleb said.

"Kaleb," Rose began, "Do you think it's wise to allow her to learn?"

He paused, staring out at the open water, the dolphins having slipped further south beyond his line of vision.

"It isn't my place to say," he replied.

"But you are her owner," Rose said.

Kaleb smiled, "You know as well as I do that isn't the case, and if I've found out one thing in my life it's that the more you try to hold someone back, the greater their desire will be to revolt. Look at the Samaya. We are perfect examples of that axiom."

"I guess the same could be said about you," Rose added.

"Indeed, my marriage to Vivian is a prime example, as you say."

"Then we must trust in the fates that brought her to us, that they had a plan other than some final conflagration between our two races," Rose offered.

A vision flashed in his mind of a hut in the desert, and the woman who'd made him promise to seek Skylla out and purchase her on the block before any other could.

"Life is never easy, my friend, and yet to this point the fates have always seen us through, so I've got to keep trusting them," Kaleb said.

Rose placed a hand on his shoulder, "That is why we trust you, Captain, because it is your heart that drives you, even if your mind is equally up to the task."

The doctor turned, and said over his shoulder, "I'll keep Parish sedated until it is no longer safe to do so."

The let us hope the *Gypsy* has the legs to make it to the shores of Yanoan, and that what we find there is more than ruins, or worse yet, Farians out for blood.

Paul was the first to call out the sighting, Charles quickly running from his seat to where Kaleb stood at the front of the bridge.

"Land, Captain!" Paul said again.

Kaleb couldn't see it, the water so close now the front window was wet with the spray of larger waves.

"Where?" Charles called up.

"Two o'clock, Captain, I'm adjusting course now," Paul replied.

Both captains turned their heads to the course and slowly a ripple of dark against the azure sea rose up along the horizon.

"We'll make it," Charles said.

"You sure?" Kaleb asked.

Charles nodded, "We've got another twenty minutes in the air if I'm correct, and ten to the beaches there if..."

He trailed off and went to the gauges beneath the navigation station, tapping some and adjusting others. Kaleb watched him a moment, heard the engines adjust and up tempo, and then looked back at the oncoming island.

Yanoan, what wonders and horrors do you hold?

"That should do it, but we won't make it too far inland, and I'll have to find a place to set her down," Charles said.

"Will she fly again?" Kaleb asked.

"I have some collectors and cyclers I can put out, but it is doubtful without a new infusion of gas,"

Nodding, Kaleb sighed and turned toward the door, saying, "Then it looks like I've got my job cut out for me."

"Once we hit land, I'll send Lance out with you. Paul and I can hold the ship, as well as take care of your man Parish," Charles offered.

Kaleb nodded before he exited to the hall. He met Stoneham just outside, the man tucking his shirt into his suspenders as he moved toward the bridge.

"Sighting?" Stoneham asked.

"Yep, looks like it won't be a water landing after all," Kaleb replied.

"Well thank the Saints for that," Stoneham said.

"We'll need everyone prepped and ready to go. You make sure Greylin is ready as well as Tolbert, and get with Lance, as he'll be with us as well," Kaleb instructed.

Stoneham gave a small salute and turned on his heel quickly heading back the way he'd come. Kaleb paused a moment in the hall, then took two steps toward Skylla's room before the door to Vivian's opened and McBrayer stepped out.

The man had on blue-tinted glasses, and his shaved head shined as though newly polished and oiled. Kaleb spied a bit of shaving lotion still on the edge of his beard just below his left ear, and the man stiffened when he saw him.

"Captain," McBrayer said.

"We've seen land, so it looks like we'll be debarking," Kaleb replied.

McBrayer nodded, "Good, it'll be nice to be off this ship."

The man moved past him, but Kaleb didn't give ground forcing the wide-shouldered McBrayer to turn sideways to get around. After the merchant had made it into his room, Kaleb went to Vivian's door and opened it without a knock.

His wife jumped at the intrusion, almost dropping a straight razor she was replacing in a wooden box. She was dressed in a nightgown, laces opened around her breasts and her hair pinned but still seductively askew on her head.

"Kaleb, are you no gentlemen?" she asked.

"I didn't know a gentleman needed to knock when entering his wife's room," Kaleb said.

She smiled, a flush coming to her cheeks. "Oh, so now I'm your wife?"

"Until the courts say otherwise, yes, and barbering for a man like McBrayer, or the saints know what else, isn't becoming a lady of your station."

She rolled her eyes and put the razor away. "Don't be jealous. McBrayer is just a friend."

"I have lots of friends, and I don't shave them with my shirt undone," Kaleb said.

"This isn't the time, Kaleb," she replied.

He pursed his lips, almost said something else, but then took a breath.

"You're right, I'll leave you to it, but get dressed as we'll be leaving the ship shortly, unless you'd like to stay here," he said.

"I didn't come all this way to wait on a ship when my father's legacy is so close," she replied.

"I figured as much, as sense never was your strong suit."

She turned on him, the flush of color returning to her cheeks but he shut the door on her, and a hiss of rage sounded through the door, but nothing else.

Stay angry, my dear, as perhaps that will get you through the upcoming journey…

Moving further down the hall, he came to Skylla's room and knocked. She opened the door in moments, her violet hair pulled back in a pony-tail and her clothes as crisp and new as if just taken from a store display in Findalynn.

"Captain," she said.

"Skylla, you look well," he replied.

She smiled and moved out of the way so that he could enter. Taking one last look down the hall at Vivian's room, he did so, Skylla shutting the door behind him.

"Any news?" she asked.

"Yes, we've seen…"

He broke off as she threw her arms around his shoulders and kissed him. Her lips were cool and a tingling sensation went from them down his spine all the way to his toes before he smelled the ocean's depths.

For a moment his hands were at his sides until he relented and pulled her close. The kiss lasted half a minute before they both broke free to catch a breath.

"What was that?" he asked.

"I'm feeling well today," she said.

It was true. She looked well, almost aglow as her skin had a rich luster and her eyes were crystalline green.

"Doc said you'd recovered nicely," he replied.

She nodded, "The wound is almost gone, and all I could think about this morning was you."

"Me?"

"Yes. There is life in you," she paused before breaking from his grasp and motioning around the room, "There is life everywhere, can't you see it?"

He looked around the small and sparsely decorated cabin.

"Not exactly," he replied.

She laughed, the sound so uncharacteristic it was strange to his ears.

"I can see the world, Kaleb, like I've never seen it before, and it is beautiful!"

"Skylla, it has to be the bands... without them."

"Without them I'm alive, even more so than the first time, and with the new blessings from the water tower I better understand how to use my gifts."

"You're scaring me," he admitted.

She turned to him, her smile fading but her eyes still aglow. Taking a step forward, she grabbed both his hands, another exchange of energy taking place with the touch.

"Don't worry, I'm still me. I'm just allowed to feel. Is that so wrong?" she asked.

He shook his head, "No."

"Then be glad, for although I spent the bulk of my power yesterday, I kept a bit, and it refills by the hour now that the bands are no longer holding it back."

"Then you can use magic?" he asked.

"A bit, but I'd need days, perhaps weeks, to refill what I've lost, but it isn't extinguished like after the duel with Ethran," she said.

He nodded, and offered her a wan smile.

"Then collect your things, as Yanoan is close and we'll be leaving the ship once we've found a place to land."

She withdrew her hands and gave him a sharp salute, "Aye Captain."

Turning to go, he took one last look at her as she strapped on her sheaf of daggers, his insides twisting at the sight.

She's changing, but I hope for the better, as I run a terrible risk allowing her to foster the magic in her blood, especially if we ever intend to return to the lands of the Samaya...

CHAPTER FIFTEEN

SKYLLA

I have been without my bands before, briefly, and the effect was a kind of emptiness as compared to the constant restraint when I had them on. Little did I understand that the hollow feeling was the result of the overuse of my Afterglow reservoir and that the feeling would have abated as that pool of energy slowly restored itself.

Now I understand the feeling, and I've kept some magic inside so that I feel the growth, like a drop of water striking the surface of a tranquil pond. It is slow, but I know it is there, growing inside me and bringing life to my body like nothing I ever knew was possible.

There is no going back, even if I am to return to the lands of the Samaya, being bound and shackled away from this power would be like strangling the very life from me. I would rather die than see that happen. This also makes me understand why my people did so rather than being forced into bondage to the Samaya.

Somehow Charles had gotten the *Gypsy* ashore, landing amid a tangle of palms that gave way to white-sand beaches broken by black volcanic rock. Tether lines had been thrown out to the surrounding trees, and the ship hovered just above the ground, the last of its gas reserves keeping it aloft, but only barely.

The crew had debarked, and Kaleb was checking packs as Greylin, Stoneham, Brett, Tolbert and Lance stood at attention. Beside them, Vivian Malett and McBrayer were outfitted for travel, Vivian actually wearing leather breeches and high boots, while McBrayer had removed his dark leather coat and wore a simple white shirt, suspenders, and a heavy ruck across his shoulders.

Charles stood at the top of the ship's entry plank watching as Paul worked to spread netting over the top of the craft for camouflage. A dozen small gas refiners hummed on the ground around the ship as they struggled to extort viable fuel from the air.

Skylla reached down and felt the grip of her break-pistol, a recent purchase at Findalynn's Powder Market, and then checked the strap of her nail-caster kept on her back next to her quiver.

Without the true weight of her clothing, the transformative robes being infinitely light, she also carried a satchel of provisions that crossed her nail-caster strap to rest on her left hip above her knives.

"That should about do it," Kaleb said.

She nodded and Stoneham raised his rifle up onto his shoulder as the rest of those in the small company went at ease.

"This map indicated a position on the island, and we'll be making for that, but we'll have to continually check our bearings as we don't know exactly where on the island we've landed. Until then be prepared for stops along the way, and keep yourself hydrated as it's hot," Kaleb said.

Those around nodded, and Kaleb had also discarded his long-coat, instead going with a button-down shirt. He wore no hat, his look almost alien to Skylla after all their years together. He too hefted a rifle, and his pack had a pry-bar strapped to it as well as his field glasses which were close at hand.

"Charles, we'll be back as soon as we can. If you don't hear from us, or the Enlightened, set off without us," Kaleb said.

Charles nodded, saying, "I'm going to work on shedding some ballast, maybe even drop an engine if necessary, and if you don't return, well, three of us might be able to get this rig back home."

Skylla noted Charles's use of "three," meaning that the captain, Doc Rose, and Paul would be making the journey as Parish would be left behind once he passed on to the Isle of Saints.

"Noted, so if you don't see us in a week, go without us," Kaleb said.

Charles nodded, and then Kaleb turned to look at the palms that led into the rocks upslope.

"Let's move," he said.

The company fell in behind him, Stoneham making conversation with Greylin as they walked. The heat of the day was oppressive, and sweat trickled down Skylla's neck after the first half hour of their journey up into the interior, bugs flying about them and rays of light piercing the canopy that stretched out emerald above their heads.

"If Yanoan's were supposed to be so advanced and powerful, why is this place so overgrown?" Greylin asked.

Brett, constantly removing his glasses to wipe fog from them, was the first to reply, "The Farians who lived here were of the elements of air and fire, and although the heat wouldn't have bothered them, the density of these lower elevation jungles would have been stifling to their air-touched side."

"So they would have lived at higher elevations," Vivian added.

"Exactly," Brett continued. "If we are to find some example of their civilization, then it will be much higher than this, and you've also got to take into account it would have been more than half a century since this island was inhabited, and jungles like this tend to quickly cover any sign of habitation that aren't extremely large structures."

They continued on, Kaleb calling for stops often, one of which was by a small waterfall where they refilled their canteens. The captain and Tolbert constantly consulted their map as Brett added advice as he could.

Skylla watched Vivian during the latest stop, the woman keeping close to McBrayer who had a large pistol in a shoulder holster that he'd fiddle with on each stop. The merchant opened the cylinder of the revolver, spun it, and then ran his large thumb over the rim and primer. At the third time he did this, she noted golden scrawls on the rim, and a short intake of breath caught in her throat.

McBrayer looked up, saw her watching him, and quickly closed the cylinder. Their eyes met a moment before Vivian said something that drew his attention.

Nul rounds, and where did you get those…

When they resumed their course, Skylla slid up the company to the lead, Kaleb wiping sweat from his brow with his sleeve as they followed a game trail through the thick undergrowth.

"McBrayer has Null rounds in his pistol," she said.

Kaleb didn't look back, his voice low as he cut away fern leaves with a machete. "You sure?"

"Yes, I saw them clearly."

"Good to know. Thanks for the heads up."

She stayed behind him and they moved another fifteen minutes before she continued, "If he has those, no telling what else he might be carrying."

"True, but at this point we'll have to wait and see, plus you'll have to remember that he's currently on our side," Kaleb said.

"Currently?"

"I'd say he'll be with us until an opportunity presents itself, but he's also far too smart to risk himself if betrayal isn't an extremely safe option."

"What about me?" she asked.

"Well, as far as he knows, you're still wearing your bands, so I'd say if we can keep that ruse up, you'd be of no more threat to him than Stoneham or myself, but be watchful nonetheless."

She nodded, "Aye, Captain."

The bands are the key, but at least that means I've now got an advantage over him for the moment...

She moved back down the procession, passing McBrayer as he helped Vivian over a tangle of rocks along the path. They didn't make eye contact this time, and she kept her distance as she moved in past Greylin who was in the rear.

"I've got our tail," she told the young man.

He nodded, readjusted his pack, and then crept further up the trail until he was behind Vivian and McBrayer. Skylla hung back, keeping Greylin's pack in her line of vision as she reached inside and touched the Afterglow there.

Against Nul rounds I've got no defense, but I know my people have developed matrices for defense so I've got to figure how they did it...

She spent the next four hours brushing against her magic and envisioning a bubble of protection around her, but nothing seemed to happen, and the Afterglow stayed steady, neither depleting or increasing during the journey.

When Kaleb called for a final halt, the party was wet, ragged, and with slumped shoulders and heads. To the west, among the mountains that ran the spine of the isle, the sun had set and long shadows mixed with the violet and pink sky to make a murky backdrop around the party.

"We'll camp here, and we'll make watches," Kaleb said.

Those around nodded, and he set a watch that didn't include either Vivian or McBrayer, although the latter offered to participate.

When they'd settled in—fern leaves cut and laid out for sleeping mats—Skylla drew close to Stoneham and shared the news of the Null rounds with him.

"You don't say," Stoneham replied.

"He must be as rich and connected as they say," she offered.

Stoneham nodded as she chewed a bit of plant she'd picked up along the way. "I don't trust him as far as I can throw him, and I'd suggest you do the same."

"I think everyone is in agreement there," she said.

"I'll have Greylin keep an eye on him as well since he's been walking behind the two all day," Stoneham added.

She looked at McBrayer, who was eating a bit of hardtack, and then at Kaleb who was breaking off bits of a biscuit and throwing it to a small creature that watched him from a low branch.

The thing was furry and similar to a raccoon, although twin feathery antennae protruded from its head and its face didn't have the distinctive grey and black mask. It caught each throw with a dexterous grab of its little paws, and she watched it turn and maneuver the bits in little fingers that were reminiscent of man, although one digit longer.

"It looks like the captain has found a friend," Stoneham said.

"It's incredible," Brett added.

The archeologist sat on the other side of her, quickly sketching away as he looked at the creature and also made notes alongside the image.

"What do you think it is?" she asked.

"Actually, I've no idea, but there are many creatures in the world we have no record of. Still…" he faded out.

Both Stoneham and Skylla turned toward him.

"Still, what?" Stoneham asked.

"Still, it seems to combine phylum, and that doesn't happen naturally, so I suspect it's a creation," Brett answered.

"Creation of what?" Stoneham continued.

"The Yanoan. It has been said that not only were they incredibly advanced with technology, they also had the power to play with the origin of species, creating beasts to serve their needs from everything like social issues to protection."

"Now you're really starting to creep me out," Stoneham said.

Skylla chuffed a laugh, but then looked back at the creature as it regarded Kaleb with polished black eyes.

If what Brett says is true, I have to wonder if you might have other strange family members in this jungle that might not be so friendly...

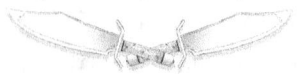

When dawn broke, Skylla rose and stretched her back, the ground having not been her ally the night before. Around the camp, others were in no better shape, the tough hike the day before, the heat, and the sleeping conditions having left everyone stiff and sore.

Kaleb, however, was already hard at work on breakfast, a small fire stoked and pot of coffee brewing. She looked at him and he wasn't sweating, his hair slicked back and a pleasant smile on his face as he hummed out some old military tune.

"What's gotten into him?" Stoneham asked, "It's like he just spent the night with you."

Skylla gave the quartermaster a sharp strike in the arm, and he winced, but smiled as well.

"Seriously, though, I feel like a runaway cart hit me, and he's singing." Stoneham said.

As Stoneham stretched, she noticed the raccoon creature was now behind Kaleb, antennae waving as it watched him work.

What are you?

"Brett, that creature. It's still here and it's now very close and watching the captain," she said.

Brett rubbed sleep from his eyes, produced his glasses and then squinted beyond Kaleb.

"Intriguing," he whispered.

"Intriguing bad or intriguing good?" she asked.

Brett shook his head, "I'm not sure, but I will say that such behavior is not found in the wild. Only a domesticated animal would stick that close to this camp for a protracted period of time, even with a constant food-source."

"Then I'm chasing it off," she said.

Grabbing her nail-caster, she took four steps toward the creature before it turned to her and began waving its antennae wildly. Kaleb stopped singing and looked up from his work.

"Skylla?" he asked.

She lifted the nail-caster, but Kaleb moved between her and the creature.

"What are you doing!" he asked.

"That creature—it's doing something to you," she warned.

He shook his head, "Yes, it's helping me!"

Furrowing her brow, she lowered the weapon slightly. "What?"

"It started… well, talking to me last night, not so much in words, but in images," Kaleb said.

By now, the entire party was up and watching the exchange. Brett, for his part had taken a book from his pack and was hurriedly leafing through it.

"What kind of images?" she asked.

"She… it, whatever, I was shown things from around the jungle, places it had seen that might interest me," he replied.

"Brett, is that possible?" she asked.

"A moment," the archeologist answered.

His voice was heightened with excitement, and the creature began to back away but Kaleb turned and spoke to it.

"Don't go. She just doesn't understand," he said.

It paused, the antennae waving back and forth as it continued to stare at her. She lowered the weapon further, the thing making no overt movements and Kaleb not taking any action against her other than defense.

"Yes," Kaleb said.

"What?" she asked.

He looked back over his shoulder, but kept his back to her, "It's asking me about you."

"Asking what?"

Kaleb took a moment to reply, "Stuff."

She was about to lift her weapon once more when Brett broke in.

"It's an Equalibrium Symbiot!" he said.

She turned, and the young scientist got to his feet, as he turned his book out so she could see it. The pages were well-worn, each panel slightly yellowed, but on one there was a sketch that roughly resembled the creature on the forest floor, as well as a half-dozen similar creatures and some text beside each. At the top of the page the words Equalibrium Symbiot was printed in bold text.

"What is it?" she asked.

Stoneham was up next to her now, as well as Tolbert.

"It is a creature created by the Enlightened to modify a person's reaction to their environment. They can take an Enlightened, say an Eldaryn fire-born, and calm his spark, keeping him in a state much like that of a Samaya, which as you can imagine has a multitude of uses," Brett said.

"Ok, so fill all us non-educated folk in," Stoneham said.

"To pass," Brett answered, then flipped the page to show another picture of a woman with one of the creatures on her shoulder. "You see, before the Final War the Enlightened used the creatures to help them breed with Samaya in hopes of assimilating the lesser species into their own ranks."

"Or to bridge the growing divide," McBrayer offered.

Everyone turned to him. The man had so few words it was strange to hear his voice, especially when defending the Enlightened.

Brett nodded, "Yes, that is possible, but whatever the reason, the Symbiots were used to help that, although they were also known to share thoughts and feelings, and above that, in extreme cases, take suffering into themselves."

"What in the name of the Saints does that mean?" Stoneham asked.

Adjusting his glasses, Brett flipped a few more pages until he read from anther passage.

"The Symbiot continue to be seen on the battlefield, their power to transfer wounds from their masters to themselves nearly doubling the ability for an Enlightened warrior to sustain his viability on the field."

Stoneham raised an eyebrow, "Well I'll be damned."

Brett nodded, "Impressive, and it seems that they desire a connection, so when this one found Kaleb…"

"It bonded somehow," Skylla said as she turned back to it.

"Which is why the captain isn't sweating, and probably why he's been singing, as the thing is regulating his body temperature as well as easing the stress of the situation."

"And a bad night's sleep," Stoneham added.

"Where can I get one?" Tolbert asked.

"Indeed, and this one seems more than eager to help." Brett said.

"It was alone, for some time. I could feel its loneliness," Kaleb said.

Everyone turned to him, and Skylla shouldered her weapon. "Well, if it has inspired you to make coffee, then I'll have to thank it."

Stoneham snickered, and Kaleb relaxed as the rest of the party eased back into a normal morning routine.

Kaleb poured everyone a cup as they came to the fire, and the Symbiot came closer, a calming purr escaping its throat as it watched everyone break their fast.

CHAPTER SIXTEEN

KALEB

I'm not really sure why this little creature chose me, but when I saw it watching from the tree I was compelled to feed it. I've never had a pet, not even in my youth because my mother hated the thought of the filth a dog would bring into the house, and she said cats were the playthings of the Enlightened.

Still, when I saw the creature, I felt an instant connection, and then after feeding it, the world changed. It was like every bit of fear, trepidation, and anxiety just fell away. They were still there, certainly, but they simply didn't matter, and the sleep I had was the most refreshing I can remember in my life.

Whatever the Enlightened did to create these creatures, I'm thankful to them for yet another gift, first Skylla, and now the Symbiot. I can only hope the creature turns out to be half as valuable to my soul as Skylla has become.

The jungle was clearing a bit as they climbed, and twice along the trail on the morning march they discovered a ruin. Each was heavily overgrown, and they looked to be dwellings, modest in size and with a kind of observatory open to the sky in the rear of each on the upper level.

Brett had collected a half-dozen small artifacts from each, and was happily discussing them with McBrayer, who kept an eye on the trinkets and the other on Vivian.

By midday the heat was intense, and they paused in a clearing along a cliff that fell away into the jungle below and provided a dramatic view of the lowlands. The Symbiot was now perched on his shoulder and he fed it bits of cracker as he watched the sky.

"A gold-note for your thoughts," Skylla said.

She sat down next to him, and he smiled at her, the dark look that Vivian gave him sliding off his mind like water on oiled steel.

"Just enjoying the afternoon," he said.

"At least someone is," she replied.

Turning, he watched as she rewound the tie for her ponytail, her violet hair wet and her brow shining with droplets of sweat.

"You know you should give it a name," she said.

"What?"

She pointed at the Symbiot, "A name, which is customary for a pet."

"Oh, he looked back and offered the creature another bite of cracker which it happily took after brushing its hands gently with its antennae.

"Do you have one in mind?" he asked.

"How about 'Hungry,'" she smiled.

"Yeah, there is that."

"Or," she continued, "You could call it Lucky, because in the case of both of you, that seems apropos."

"Lucky, huh, that makes…"

He trailed off, the creature pausing mid bite as a wave of terror washed over him.

"What is it?" Skylla asked.

"There's something out there," he said, turning back to the jungle.

Skylla had just enough time to draw her nail-caster when the jungle exploded and a thing twice the size of a tiger and green as lake algae nearly took the head off Greylin who luckily fell backward at the oncoming rush.

Stoneham cried out for Tolbert to get his rifle, and McBrayer put his large frame between the beast and Vivian.

"Brett!" Kaleb yelled a warning.

After the beast missed Greylin, it turned toward Brett, the archeologist standing dumbstruck in the middle of the camp.

Skylla fired a two-foot titanium shaft into the creature's shoulder, and it turned and roared a challenge, falling back a step as Tolbert threw Stoneham his rifle and Greylin pulled Brett out of the thing's path.

Skylla's shot had drawn the creature's full attention, and it pressed low to the ground as a chest-shaking growl rumbled between four dagger-long teeth and two dozen smaller ones.

Kaleb drew his pistol and fired off a quick shot, the round striking the thing in the skull but bouncing off with only a tear in the fur trailing a bit of blood.

It roared again and sprang, both he and Skylla jumping to opposite sides of the attack as the creature slid close to the cliff edge, claws leaving marks on the stone before it stopped.

Another shot sounded, Stoneham firing his rifle and the beast let out another roar as it struck at Skylla with a huge paw but she rolled out of the way just in the nick of time.

Firing a second time, Kaleb aimed for the ribcage, and this time the round missed a rib and penetrated, but the beast shook like it was a bee sting and leapt again, this time directly on Skylla.

She managed to get her nail-caster up and send another nail into the thing's enormous chest, but then it was on her, claws tearing at her jacket and mouth coming down to pierce her throat.

She managed to get her weapon between its jaws but the claws tore at her, blood splattering the stone. Without thinking, Kaleb charged, his full weight and momentum slamming into the beast's side.

It felt like he struck a street-cart filled with bags of grain, but somehow he moved it, the beast falling off her and Stoneham sending another round into its open mouth that put it in a clawing fit. The creature struck at its own mouth, back legs going close to the cliff edge as rocks tumbled down behind it.

Kaleb recovered enough to raise his pistol and fan the hammer, three more rounds slamming into the beast's face before it retreated another step and the cliff gave way. A terrible roar followed it down, and then the sound of rending branches came up over the lip until a final thud sounded. Moments later a half dozen birds took flight from below.

Kaleb knelt beside Skylla. Her breathing was heavy and her face pale as her exposed abdomen lay open in six long gashes where the claws had racked her.

"Skylla?" Kaleb whispered.

Her eyes were open, but she stared at that sky.

"Skylla, can you hear me?"

"A moment," she whispered, "Give me a moment."

His hands were shaking, and he felt the Symbiot in his mind, drawing off the top layer of his emotions, but it couldn't deaden the horror of those gashes. As he looked at them, he blinked, the ragged edges having a fine layer of shimmer on them.

"What?" he murmured.

He trailed off, the glow continuing until the wounds were no more than scratches along the skin that bled slightly but were otherwise far from lethal.

Skylla blinked, then tried to sit up but swooned, and he caught her head before it struck the stone beneath.

"I feel the magic, but it is gone now," she whispered.

I have no idea how we won the war...

"It's incredible," he replied shaking his head.

Stoneham was to them both an instant later, rifle still raised as he first looked over the edge and then back at Skylla.

"Damn lucky that, Saint Erik must have been with you to leave only scratches," the quartermaster said.

Kaleb nodded, and Skylla was now breathing steadily, although she stayed against the stone and he pulled out a canteen to press it to her lips.

"Take this," he offered.

She sipped and then drank more fully, her hair wet against the grey cliff beneath her, but her cheeks had regained some color.

"That may have been some luck," Brett said, "But the sound of your weapons seems to have brought other company."

Kaleb looked up, and Brett was pointing to the sky to the east where a ship hung along the horizon.

"Enlightened," Stoneham hissed.

"They've followed us," Greylin added.

Kaleb reached to his side and pulled his field glasses from the strap, lifting them to his eyes. The lenses adjusted, and he got a better view of the ship, a half-dozen glowing outlines of elemental essence visible from its open galley.

"It's one of the two from the island," he said.

"Then we need to move, get under the cover of the trees," Brett said.

Kaleb looked down at Skylla. She'd opened her eyes and was looking to the east as well.

Was it the sound of the guns or the use of your magic that brought them?

"The trees are growing less dense as we move higher, so hiding will be more difficult," Stoneham said.

Kaleb nodded, "Agreed, but we have to move, so let's get to it."

He stowed his glasses and offered Skylla his hand. She took it, and he sensed no magic in the touch, instead her hand cold and unfeeling as any Samaya.

"Can you walk?" he asked.

"Yes," she replied.

"Greylin, get the field dressing, we'll wrap her wounds and then head inland," Kaleb ordered.

The party began preparations, and Greylin brought out the medical kit. Kaleb stood, watching the horizon a moment before an image flashed in his mind. It was a bridge and a road beyond, somewhere further up in the heights but it felt like an old friend.

Thank you, he thought.

A warm feeling swept over him, and even in the face of the oncoming Enlightened he smiled.

The party moved higher and higher while sticking to the trees as much as possible. The heights were a tangle of sheer cliffs, jagged rocks, and jungle hanging onto any viable land it could. Kaleb stopped periodically to bring his field glasses up and check the horizon. Each time the Enlightened ship was closer to their previous position.

They must have lost us for the moment, either that or the aftereffects of Skylla's magic is drawing them like bees to honey...

He led them on, each turn of the course somehow familiar, and the party followed without comment, although Stoneham and Skylla whispered on occasion. 'Lucky' now rested on his shoulder, and the creature was warm and comforting there, the antennae waving as they moved beneath the canopy.

Within an hour, the Enlightened ship hung above the cliff where the battle had taken place, ropes dangling from its belly as figures slid down to look at the area. He watched through the binoculars and took a small sip from his nearly empty canteen.

"What does it look like, Captain?" Stoneham asked.

"They've landed and are checking the cliff were they creature fell," he replied.

"Well, at least we have a lead on them," the quartermaster said.

Kaleb nodded, "True, but if they debark to follow us, they'll be moving at speed, and with Skylla wounded and Vivian being Vivian, they'll cut that lead quickly."

Stoneham hefted his rifle and patted two shells on his ammunition belt.

"Well, at least two of them won't be going back to their island," he said.

"There is that," Kaleb nodded.

Vivian walked up, McBrayer behind her a half dozen steps. "What do you see?" she asked.

"The Enlightened are debarking at the cliff," he replied.

She put a hand over her eyes and looked down the slopes toward the dark shape of the ship.

"Here," he offered her the glasses.

Taking them, she held them up and watched as Kaleb cast a look a McBrayer. The man wiped his bald head with a handkerchief, his dark blue glasses keeping his eyes shaded from view.

"What is that?" Vivian asked.

Kaleb looked down the slope but couldn't make anything out. Vivian dropped the glasses into his outstretched hand and he brought them up.

The ship came into view, and a cage hung from it, some kind of beast moving back and forth inside.

"Brett!" Kaleb called.

The archeologist was holding a conversation with Greylin when he looked up adjusting his spectacles.

"Captain?"

"Get up here," Kaleb replied.

The young man stowed a book in his lap and move quickly up the path to where the others stood. Kaleb handed him the glasses, and he removed his spectacles before bringing them to his eyes.

"Incredible," he whispered.

"What is it?"

"Oh, that these glasses can see elemental energy," Brett answered.

Kaleb frowned, "No, what's in the cage?"

"Well," he paused a bit and then added, "It looks like bones and sticks."

"May I?" McBrayer asked.

Brett lowered the glasses, looked at Kaleb who nodded, and then handed them to McBrayer. The man took a long look before sighing.

"Dweoller," he said.

Brett took the glasses back, shaking his head, "Those are only legend."

"I've seen one, in Tiefon for the World Expo half a decade ago," McBrayer replied.

"What's a Dweoller?" Stoneham asked.

Brett cut McBrayer off from answering, adding his own opinion, "They are constructs, tracking hounds made by the Enlightened to find people or items that contain Afterglow."

"Then they'll have our trail for sure," Stoneham said.

"Unless I leave the party," Skylla offered.

Everyone turned to look at her. She'd walked up behind them, Greylin at her side and an arm covering the bandages at her waist.

"That's not going to happen," Stoneham said even before Kaleb could get the words out.

"He's right, we're in this together, and there is strength in numbers," Kaleb added.

"Then we should get moving," McBrayer said.

The man adjusted the pistol strapped beneath his left arm and then helped Vivian down from the rocks they'd been using for the view.

Skylla looked at him, her green eyes almost pleading, but he smiled and shook his head, saying, "Greylin, stick close to Skylla."

"Sir," Greylin replied.

The party formed another line and he led them on. After another half hour, a series of buildings came into view. They were more ruins than true structures at this point, but it was the first true settlement they'd seen.

All were made of stone, but shattered glass lay among the tangles of ferns, and vines crept over the surface of oddly angled walls. The streets were set at angles as well, the entire space taking on the aspect of giant triangles laid against each other, one over the next.

It took less than two minutes to find the first impact crater. It was ten feet deep and tumble-down with vegetation, but there was no mistaking it.

"They were bombed," Stoneham said.

"It was a war," Kaleb replied.

He didn't look back a Skylla, instead keep his focus on leading them through the ruins. The further they went in, the greater the level of destruction, some buildings reduced to no more than piles of rubble and old ash.

"I don't get it. If the Yanoan were here, and Malett bombed them, why secret his ship away on their tomb?" Stoneham asked.

"It would be the perfect place to hide a ship the size of the *Glaive*, assuming you were confident no Yanoans remained," Brett offered.

"Well if there were, you can rest assured they'd have taken out a reprisal for this damage on any craft abandoned here," Greylin said.

Kaleb looked back. The young man rarely spoke, and it was both good and a little disturbing to hear him join in the conversation. His namesake, Greylin Motherborn, was certainly the most famous Samaya in history, and the first Tome-Mage his people could lay claim to in the time before history was readily recorded and demons still walked the face of the world.

From somewhere in the jungles behind them a howl split the air and the hairs on the back of Kaleb's neck stood on end.

Stoneham came around with his rifle at the ready, and McBrayer drew his pistol.

"What was that?" Vivian asked.

"It was the Dweoller, and it's close," Brett replied.

Kaleb drew his pistol and then fell back a step, calling, "Come on, we're close!"

The party turned and followed as he picked up the pace, Stoneham asking, "Close to what?"

Kaleb didn't reply, and kept moving, the angles of the streets enough to make travel extremely confusing but the visions in his head grew stronger and he made every turn as though it was his home town.

Greylin's rifle sounded from the rear, and a half-dozen fiery darts splattered the stones close to Kaleb as he ducked behind a crumbling wall. Stoneham pressed in next to him, followed by Skylla, and they all crouched lower as a ball of fire burst over their heads showering the field with bits of blue flame.

One of the fire droplets struck Stoneham on the leg and he howled before Skylla smothered it with a fold of fabric that extended from her coat.

"Thanks," Stoneham said.

Kaleb inspected the wound, and the skin was blistered and black in a perfect circle half-way up the man's shin.

"I'll live," Stoneham forced a smile.

"At least for the moment," Skylla said, peaking up over the wall.

Kaleb did the same, another round firing from Greylin's rifle as he saw the young man hunkered down with Lance and Tolbert to his right. McBrayer, Vivian, and Brett knelt behind a half-wall to his left. Further into the ruins behind, figures were moving, and one who was no larger than an eight-year old with blue hair was holding a ball of orange flame in his hands.

"Great, there's an Eldaryn pyromancer," Kaleb said.

Skylla nodded, adding, "And I saw one of them flying between buildings, so they've got at least one Aspara with them as well."

Kaleb shouted to his right, "Greylin! We're no more than a hundred yards from a bridge, so try to keep their heads down while we fall back!"

The young man nodded and then took another shot. Beside Kaleb, Stoneham chambered a Null round and then turned, "I'll get the pyromancer, as that fire will be the death of us all."

Kaleb slipped around the quartermaster until he was next to Skylla. "Can you run?" he asked.

"Yes."

"Good," he pointed down another angled street, "Take this until the first right turn, then head across the bridge."

"But..."

He cut her off, "That's an order."

Stoneham rose up and leveled his rifle, Kaleb giving Skylla one last serious look before he pulled his pistol and ran toward Vivian's position.

Two shots rang out as he ran, and from the far side of the battlefield a fireball bloomed that sent a wave of heat washing over him before he leapt behind the Vivian's cover.

"Looks like your quartermaster is a hell of a shot," McBrayer said.

Kaleb looked up over the lip of the wall, orange flames still burning around an enormous black circle where the Eldaryn once stood.

"I guess the little guy couldn't control the fireball once the Null round hit him," Kaleb said.

"Looks that way," McBrayer added.

"What now?" Vivian asked.

Kaleb checked his cylinder, than pointed back the way he came. "That road there. It moves down a piece before another road intersects it from the right. If you take that you'll come to a bridge where Skylla will meet you."

"The Enlightened?" Brett asked.

"McBrayer and I will keep them at bay, so both of you run on my mark," Kaleb said.

Counting down, he hit one and then he and McBrayer came up over the wall and each fired a round. Across the way, Greylin did the same, one of the shots striking a defensive matrix and causing it to flair brightly.

Vivian and Brett ran back to where Stoneham held the middle and then disappeared from sight.

"Do you really think it's a good idea sending them alone?" McBrayer asked.

"Better than being here at the moment," Kaleb said.

As if on cue a rolling wave of wind rose up, debris cast about them like a thousand cutting blades.

"Fall back!" Kaleb screamed.

He got to his feet, shielding his eyes as a dozen stings hit him all over his body, but he still managed to move back toward Stoneham. McBrayer was beside him, and then came another scream from his left as Lance was pulled down by the Dwoeller.

The beast was little more than a black blur in the torrent, but it's boney skull thrashed from side to side furiously. Kaleb took another step, blood caught on the wind splattering his cheek as he raised his voice again, "Follow me!"

Greylin was beside him, then Tolbert, with Stoneham taking up the rear as they slipped further from the apex of the wind. When Kaleb could finally unshield his eyes they were half way down the street to the turn, and he increased his pace as Stoneham drew out his final Null round and chambered it.

"That thing was fast!" Greylin said.

The young man's face was pale, and Tolbert looked no better beside him, flying debris having opened a wound on his forehead and his right shoulder was charred where fire had found purchase.

"Just keep moving," Kaleb said.

They did so, but Kaleb fell back until he was beside Stoneham, saying, "Keep them moving across the bridge, and once you're across, I want you to set the charges."

Stoneham nodded and moved on.

That's what I love about you Stoneham, you never argue or divert, and that is all a commander can ask…

Once Stoneham was around the turn, Kaleb stopped and looked back, the wind-wall was still intact and moving forward.

So what is your next move…

As if in answer, a shape appeared in the wind and leapt out onto the street with a clatter of wood and bones' claws. The Dwoeller was larger than a man, perhaps the girth of a bear, and no more than a tangle of vines and bone that created overly long front legs. It's head was a bestial skull, with eyes that were empty sockets save a darkness that drew in the light.

Around the thing's fangs blood and flesh still dripped, but Kaleb held his ground in the face of it, the calm of "Lucky" deflecting the terror.

Expelling his pistol's cylinder, he reached down and plucked out the spent casing, the Dwoeller lowering its head and then charging. It bounded down the rubble-strewn road, each leap twice the length of a running man's gait.

Kaleb reached into his belt, drew out his final Null round and thumbed it into the cylinder. With a quick snap, he slid the cylinder back into place, pulled back the hammer, and raised the weapon.

The Dweoller leapt, and it was so close he could see the intricate ruins etched into each bone and piece of wood as well as the platinum wire that attached all the pieces together. There was a moment of clarity, and then he pulled the trigger.

The Null round caught the beast directly in the skull, the anti-magic shattering the bone in two before Kaleb side-stepped and the lifeless body sailed past. When it struck the ground, bits of bone and wood broke away, the platinum wire turning molten like a lit fuse before the entire thing crumbled into an unrecognizable heap.

"Thanks, Lucky," he said.

Lucky trilled on his shoulder, the calm the thing instilled him in bolstered by a sense of pride.

The feeling was short-lived as a lance of air ripped down the length of the street tossing debris to either side before striking him full in the chest.

The blow picked him up and cast him back a dozen feet like a rag doll. The effect of the blast was like striking water from a height in an improper dive, the surface becoming solid from the speed of impact.

Pain shot through him, both from the impact of the air blast and also his contact with the ground after the blow. He struggled to breathe, stars swimming in his eyes and his ears ringing.

This is it then...

Just as quickly as the strike itself, the pain abated, and he drew in a huge breath of air like a man surfacing after a forced length beneath the waves. He blinked, sat up, and clutched at his chest but found it intact and well.

"How?" he whispered.

He looked right and left, his pistol some feet away at the spot where he'd been struck, but it was "Lucky" that finally drew his attention.

The little creature lay next to him on his left, and it wheezed as it struggled to breathe, a trickle of blood coming from its small mouth.

"No..." he whispered.

Leaning over, he gently picked Lucky up and then caught movement from his peripheral vision as men with blades and bows came into view further up the street.

"I've got you," he said.

Standing, he pulled Lucky to his chest and turned to flee, his feeling of calm gone as a dull emptiness settled into his mind.

CHAPTER SEVENTEEN

SKYLLA

The magic is gone once more, the reservoir empty and a hollowness like a thousand years alone settling into my being. Once you taste what the Afterglow has to offer, how it warms your inside, there is no going back, and yet I've lost it again.

This time, however, I spent all I had and asked for no more, whatever connection to the Afterglow Sea I managed in the duel with Kaleb not possible today, even as I struggled to bind my own wounds.

Now the robes hang weighty on my shoulders, and the world seems dull and dark, but I live, and in time the power will return, even if more slowly than a single drop a day onto the parched landscape of my Wizard's soul.

Stoneham limped away from the edge of the bridge, his hands rolling out a fuse as Greylin pulled himself up over the rocky lip beneath the span with the help of Brett and Tolbert. Vivian and McBrayer had fallen back to the first line of triangular buildings. Skylla waited at the verge, her nail-caster in hand and eyes on the far side.

Where are you?

As if in answer, Kaleb, covered in dust and debris appeared amid the tangle of buildings. He was running and carried something in his arms.

"Stoneham, you'd better be ready!" she called.

"I'm working on it!"

She looked back at Greylin who had made it up and was running with the other two younger men toward the building where Vivian and her consort now crouched low.

"Greylin, take a position there," she pointed. "And have that rifle ready."

The young man stopped, diverted his course to a clump of grass and stone and then took cover.

At least he listens, you've got to like that...

Looking back at the bridge, she raised her weapon and watched as Kaleb ran across, men with blazing weapons coming into view behind him.

"The bowman!" she called.

Greylin fired a shot, and further behind Kaleb a matrix flared but protected the Enlightened within from the shot.

Damnable defenses...

One of the bowman fired an arrow, and the flaming blue head cut a burning wound in Kaleb's right shoulder as the narrowly missed a direct hit.

She cursed, but Stoneham was on a knee next to her and fired his rifle again, his final Null round taking the closest archer in the chest and dropping him.

Kaleb kept moving, and she scanned for other enemies but no one came into range of her weapon before he made it to the other side.

"You're wounded," she said.

Kaleb shook his head, "I'll live, but Lucky..."

He held out the symbiot, the creature lifeless in his hands. Before she could say anything, Stoneham called out. "You want this down?"

"Do it," Kaleb answered.

Stoneham produced a lighter and caught the fuse. The flaring tip moved away quickly and they all fell back, Greylin joining them as they ducked into the first line of buildings.

Skylla turned back, the figure of the Aspara appearing on the far side of the bridge just before a thunderous report of explosives shook the span. The construction groaned and then gave way, a full third of it dropping away into the oblivion of the chasm that separated the two sides of the town.

One the far side, amid a haze of dust, the Aspara floated. Their enemy was a woman, tall and lean, with skin like milk-slacked chocolate and black hair that fell in a waving cascade of braids.

"That should hold them a bit," Stoneham said.

The Aspara treaded closer, her feet still off the ground, but everyone on their side raised weapons and she floated away before raising her hand. Behind her, one of the bowmen launched a flare of yellow light into the sky from his palm, and Kaleb let out a curse.

"Their bringing in their ship," he said.

"What about the Dweoller. Can they still track us?" Vivian asked.

Kaleb shook his head, "No, I took care of it."

Skylla turned to him, the symbiot still held in his arms.

"What happened?" she asked.

He reached around, pulled his leather pack from where it rested on his hip, and gently placed the animal inside it.

"It saved me," he replied.

No one asked anything further, and Kaleb sighed before returning his attention to the party.

"We continue upward from here, and I've got a feeling we're close," he said.

"How do you know that?" Brett asked.

"I had a vision," he replied.

With that, he moved toward a breech in the wall at the back of the building, the rest of the party following him.

Their path led them through the remainder of the town, then up a foliage-covered road into the heights. From below, they saw the airship come for the Enlightened, the thing tethering itself to the far side of the chasm as the advance party re-boarded.

They stayed to the trees and kept low as the ship passed over them twice, but after the second pass it crept skyward until it was only a dot in the blue.

"They'll stay there, watching with spy glasses, until we come out of cover and they'll then descend like a bird of prey," Stoneham said.

Kaleb nodded, "True, but we've only got an hour of sunlight left, and once it goes down we've got a better chance of slipping away."

Skylla looked to the horizon, the clouds spread out in pink waves against the fading light of the evening. From this position, the view was dramatic.

I wonder what it was like to live here, and what peace these people must have once known...

She continued to watch the sky go dark as Greylin bandaged Kaleb's wound from the bridge, as well as those of the other members of the party. By the time the stars lit the night sky and the Ghost Moon hung heavy to the west, a somber silence had fallen over them all. Stoneham slept and Brett rocked back and forth with his arms around his knees.

Vivian lay next to McBrayer who watched the sky with his pistol in his lap while Tolbert and Greylin played a quiet game of Zhot, the duo choosing between parchment, stone, and sheers after a soft count to three.

A chill was in the air at their height, and she shivered until her clothing crawled on her skin and covered her completely, a grey undergarment covering her stomach and arms.

"A very nice trick," Kaleb said.

He slid in next to her, his field glasses around his neck and his satchel left behind where he'd been sleeping as well.

"The clothing is a wonder, to be sure," she replied.

"And how does it feel to be a Wizard?" he asked.

The question gave her pause, and she turned to regard him in the moonlight. He'd lost the glow from the previous day, but the soft light helped smooth the tired lines around his eyes, and the dirt from the battle gave him a rugged look.

Perhaps I've grown too fond of seeing you road-weary, but it makes you all the more real and valiant in my eyes...

"I'm no Wizard," she said.

"You know that isn't true,"

Frowning, she went back to looking at the sky, saying, "I'm not sure what I am, but Wizard isn't at the top of my list."

"You can wield the Afterglow," he said.

"Yes, but my control is limited, and each time I turn around I've somehow managed to lose my power."

"Is it gone now?" he asked.

She closed her eyes and took a deep breath.

Empty, like the inside of a can of oil that's been wiped with a rag, only a light sheen of that liquid left to slick a testing finger.

"Yes."

He nodded, and mirrored her sigh. "It will return in time."

"Is that a good thing?" she asked.

"Meaning?"

She turned back to him, "Meaning, now that I've controlled what I can do, even if only slightly, I can't put the bands back on."

Kaleb stared at her for a moment and then nodded, "I know, as I could see it in your eyes when you came out of the tower."

"Then I suppose my time on the *Tyger* is done," she said.

He shook his head, "Are you crazy? What would make you say that?"

"Because you can't have a free Enlightened on the ship."

Reaching out, he touched the fabric at her wrists, his fingers sliding over the material like it was metal. "If you can mimic the bands, then I know that every member of the crew will support you staying. We are a family, and we never, ever, abandon each other."

Biting her lip she nodded.

I can't cry, and as much as I'd like to throw my hands around his neck, I've got to resist that as well…

"Good, then just keep working at what you were born to do, and let me worry about how we get away with you doing it," he said.

She was about to reply, but he got to his feet and called back to the camp, "We've got to move."

The party stirred, and Kaleb took one last look at the sky with his field glasses and then retrieved his pack.

Standing, Skylla readied her nail-caster and then followed the party into the dark as Kaleb led them on.

An hour had passed as they continued to climb, Kaleb periodically checking the sky before he'd have them move on. It was slow going in the dark, even with the moonlight giving some illumination as they kept to shadows.

More ruins dotted the landscape, and they had to turn back twice when their path came to a sheer rock face going up hundreds of feet above them. On the third such trip to the face, however, they discovered a hole had been cut into the rock and a rusted door was set into the wall.

"What do you make of it?" Kaleb asked.

"It's not like the rest of the architecture we've seen, as the Yanoan's had no doors I could make out other than wood," Brett replied.

The young man was pale and jumpy, but he held it together enough to give opinion when asked.

"Stoneham, can you open in?" Kaleb asked.

Stoneham pulled off his pack and removed a pry bar from where it was strapped on the outside.

"I'll see what I can do," the quartermaster said.

He brought Greylin up and the two of them began working on the lock. The rest of the party sat down, took some water, and waited, the noise of the two working putting everyone on edge. An hour passed, then two, the curses from Stoneham echoing up against the cliff face as Kaleb kept his field glasses on the night sky as the Blood Moon rose behind the Ghost and started chasing it from the sky.

By the third hour, Kaleb called Stoneham to a halt, the man covered in sweat and rock dust with Greylin in no better shape.

"What's the word?" Kaleb said.

Stoneham wiped his brow, "Well, she's not going to open on her own, but I've made enough of a hole I could get a stick or two of dynamite in there and we can blow her open."

Kaleb nodded, looked up into the sky, and then said to the group, "Everyone fall back, we're going to blow the door."

"Is that wise, Captain Cross? You don't even know what is behind it and surely such an explosion will draw the Enlightened down on us," McBrayer said.

"That's true, but we've got no choice. The night won't last forever, and this wall must be part of an upper plateau, so I'm betting this door leads to some kind of interior structure."

"But it might only be a bomb shelter, and if so we'll be caught for sure," McBrayer continued.

"Sometimes, you've got to have faith," Kaleb said.

McBrayer bristled, but Vivian touched his arm and he shook his head before stalking off.

"You'd better be right," she said before following the trader.

Kaleb nodded and then gave Stoneham the go. The quartermaster took more explosives from his pack and began testing sticks. Unlike the bridge, Greylin ran the fuse and Stoneham set the charge, and once everything was in place they all ducked behind cover as Stoneham lit the fuse.

Less than a minute later an explosion split the pre-dawn calm, and Skylla rose from behind a rock to see a cloud of dust turning the dusky world to complete shadow.

"Torches!" Kaleb called.

Brett, Greylin, and Tolbert all produced cylinder lights, the beams cutting through the settling debris until they could see the door was gone and a dark hole led further into the cliff face.

Kaleb looked up with this field glasses, his lips pursing once before he called them all to move.

Skylla's gaze went up as well, the breaking light of morning blazing just below the horizon to the east. There, with pink clouds above, she searched for movement, but nothing stood out.

I'm sure you've seen us, but I pray you stay where you are because I don't want to have to kill more of my people tonight...

CHAPTER EIGHTEEN

KALEB

The calm has fled, replaced instead by a dread that each decision I make is one step closer to oblivion. I don't know what we will find behind this door, but I've few other options open to me.

Somewhere up in these rocky climbs the SkyGlaive is supposed to rest, and if the Yanoans were working underground during the end days of the war, then perhaps Malett repurposed their secure base as the last resting place of his famed dreadnaught.

Why do I think that? Because that is exactly what I'd have done if I was going to hide a weapon from a world gone mad with the desire to use it.

The passage was on a slight incline as they moved up it. Greylin led the way, his light shining on stone walls that were neither hand-carved or natural, but instead a smooth run that spoke of Kin molding craftsmanship.

They moved for the better part of twenty minutes up the incline, legs burning, until they came to a circular stair. Again, the stone was shaped, and Brett marveled aloud several times at the ability of the Enlightened to work with their environment before they came to another door.

This one was much the same as the first, almost an afterthought of Samayan design, but there was no lock, just a release bar that groaned with rusty protest as they threw it.

The sound echoed down the stair and Stoneham cursed under his breath.

"Again, this isn't Enlightened work, but looks to have been added later," Brett said.

"You might be as lucky as I've heard, Captain Cross," McBrayer said.

The man's words were veiled, but in the close confines they carried to all ears, and Kaleb smiled.

"Saint Erik must be looking over me," he replied.

Stoneham chuffed a laugh as he opened the door, the hall beyond home to a dozen doors. Moving inside, they closed the door, and Stoneham pulled a hammer and chisel from his pack before he drove the chisel between the frame and door as a wedge.

While he worked, Greylin and Brett moved up the hall to the doors, their lights showing a series of small stores that had long ago been emptied other than scattered and broken debris.

"Must have been some kind of reserve storerooms," Tolbert said.

"Probably, and located at a back exit just in case the main entry was blocked," Kaleb replied.

Once Stoneham was done, and the rooms were cleared, the party moved on, the next hall leading up another flight of stairs and beneath an arch. Here, a kind of annex existed with a series of halls leading off of it in five directions.

"Any ideas?" Kaleb asked.

Brett had moved to a wall by one of the exits, his fingers moving over the stone to reveal an inscription in the stone. After brushing the dust from each symbol, he took out his book and began flipping pages. Tolbert held the light for him, and before Brett could find reference the Mage-Tech spoke up.

"It is a sign. This hall leads to the labs," Tolbert said.

Brett looked up and adjusted his glasses, asking, "You speak Enlightened?"

Tolbert shook his head, "No, but I read Tech Glyphs, and that is what these are."

Brett looked back at the etching, "Of course! It makes perfect sense that Tech Glyphs would have descended from Enlightened teachings, especially those of Yanoan engineers!"

"Thanks for the history lesson, Professer," Stoneham began, "but do any of these lead to a larger area?"

Tolbert moved around the circle, brushing dust from the inscriptions until he stopped at the third one.

"Fabrication Bay," he said.

"Sounds good to me," Stoneham said.

Kaleb nodded, and the party moved down that hall. The passage twisted and turned twice around rooms that were filled with raw materials, mostly rusted iron, before finally opening into a much larger chamber.

Moonlight filtered into the cavern from squares cut in the ceiling that shown down in pillars of silver. The room was massive, perhaps three times the size of a standard Dragmarsh military hanger, and the bulk of it rested in shadow other than the center where the moonlight shafts fell down in a line.

Just in the outline of the line several Samayan military sleds sat next to a large stack of crates, and something the size of a small cottage covered in a tarp.

"Captain…" Skylla whispered.

He turned and followed her line of sight. Lurking above them, deep in the shadows to the left side of the light shafts was the hulk of something half the size of the hanger and a third its width.

"The SkyGlaive," he whispered.

Brett was beside him, also looking up, and added, "It's huge."

Kaleb shook his head and then turned his attention back to the party. "Stoneham, you and Brett find a way to open this vault, because if the ship got in here, there has to be way out. Everyone else, come with me."

The party broke up, Stoneham and Brett moving away from the ship and the rest of them running toward a series of risers inset into the cavern wall, each connected with steel ladders. Above those, a large plank stretched over the gap between the wall and the *Glaive*.

Kaleb's shoulder was aching, but he kept moving upward, Skylla at his side and Greylin leading the way with rifle in hand.

"Damn long climb," Kaleb said.

Skylla looked back at him with a frown but said nothing, Tolbert huffing behind and the ring of Vivian's well-heeled boots echoing up into the darkness above as she and McBrayer brought up the rear.

"Tolbert, how long to get the ship moving?" Kaleb asked.

Tolbert shook his head, "No idea captain. She may not move at all if there are no elemental cores inside her."

"The ship doesn't use cores, it has an arcane furnace," McBrayer offered.

Kaleb looked back, as did Tolbert, the merchant's bald head shining with sweat even in the gloom.

It seems Vivian has more knowledge of her father's affairs than I'd thought, and she's also not shy about sharing...

"Does that make a difference to you, Mr. Tolbert?" Kaleb asked.

"Maybe, but I'll have to get to the engine room nonetheless, and this ship..." he trailed off.

Kaleb followed the mage-tech's gaze, the mass of the *Glaive* now in full view beside them. It was a gargantuan frame, blue-white beneath and deeper grey-blue above with twin jet engines, one aft and one fore, mirrored on either side of the lower hull. The shell of the ship was made of some kind of fibrous plating that shown in the dim light, and the under-structure was metallic with oricalcum overlays that swirled like moving clouds along the surface. There were observation nodes fore and aft as well, and hidden gun emplacements could be made out beneath the fiber sheeting along the entirety of the hull.

"She's got to be eight hundred feet long," Tolbert said.

"A thousand," Kaleb corrected, "And she's got twin ballast pods running along her upper shell which means she'll have a command gondola above as well as below."

They continued on, each step bringing them closer to the rusted metal bridge that led from the hanger risers into the *Glaive's* lower gondola. Skylla was the first to make it, pushing past Greylin until her boot tested the metal. From further away in the vault, the sound of metal gears grinding into action echoed through the enormous hanger and they all turned to look.

As if in response to the sound, a shaft of brilliant morning light broke through the gloom and the epic form of the *Glaive* glittered as the oricalcum blazed with white-gold light.

"It's like the ship's alive," Tolbert said.

"As much as magic is alive, Mr. Tolbert, and I can sense the power in her like the warmth off a fire," Skylla replied.

"But the better question would be, can you use that magic?" Kaleb asked.

Skylla smiled back, her skin having turned a fine green and her eyes sparkling with a glow of the new dawn.

"It looks that way," she said.

"Good, then if you see any of the Enlightened following us, be sure to make them think twice," he said.

"Aye, captain," she replied.

Kaleb moved up and past her, his boots clanking on the bridge as his gaze drifted below to the dark holes in the hanger where other entrances opened to the vault.

"Greylin, stick with me!" Kaleb called.

The young man's steps echoed on the steel behind him as they made their way over to the ship. The entry was an open metal door, the hinges coated with dust over a thick layer of grease.

"It looks like they prepared her for a long delay," Kaleb whispered.

"Sir?" Greylin asked.

"Nothing, just keep that rifle handy in case there are automatons in this thing," Kaleb replied.

Greylin nodded and the two moved inside. The interior was dark, the hall leading deeper into the bulk of the huge craft and away from the ever growing ambient light of the exterior.

Kaleb turned around but light burst into existence above his head, a series of lamps pulsing with a warm yellow glow.

"How?" he asked.

Tolbert was at the door, one hand on a gem placed into the frame of the portal that glowed with the same yellow light.

"Looks like power is still active, Captain, so whatever source they are using hasn't abated or been deactivated," Tolbert said.

Kaleb nodded and then led the party further inside, the entry breaking left and right as it led fore and aft with a multitude of doors on either side.

"Any ideas?" Kaleb asked.

Tolbert moved up, his gaze going back and forth down the long hall.

"Aft," he finally said.

"Why?" Kaleb asked.

"There will be lower quarters here, weapons stations, and even auxiliary control, but the main bridge will be above us, and any elevator will be toward the rear, as will any power station," Tolbert answered.

Nodding, Kaleb motioned Greylin down the corridor and followed with his pistol at the ready. Half way down the hall to the rear, Greylin stopped for a moment and motioned for them all to advance.

"Looks promising," Greylin said.

Kaleb's gaze followed the young man's finger to a door with a seam down the middle and two dusty glass portholes.

"That would be the elevator, Captain. You should go on up," Tolbert said.

"What about you?"

The mage-tech smiled, "I've got to get to the engines and see if I can fire them up. We may have limited power now, but we'll need those engines primed and pumping if we want to move this beast."

Kaleb nodded and Tolbert moved on.

"Greylin, you go with him, and if he gets the engines going, come back here and then head up to find me on the bridge unless there's trouble, then find a gunnery station," Kaleb ordered.

Greylin nodded and moved after Tolbert, Kaleb turning to McBrayer and Vivian. His mouth fell when only McBrayer stared back at him.

"Where is Vivian?" Kaleb asked.

McBrayer shrugged, but didn't reply.

Bastard, you're damn lucky I don't just shoot you for holding your tongue at a time like this…

A hissing curse slipped Kaleb's lips but he moved to the seamed door, found another crystal set in the frame beside it and ran his hand over the surface. A light pulsed inside and the doors opened.

"After you," Kaleb said.

McBrayer moved inside and Kaleb followed, his hand finding another crystal and waving over it. A moment later and the elevator was moving up through the superstructure of the craft, McBrayer humming a quiet tune as the sound of chugging metal rolling against metal droned on outside.

"Do you always sing at times like this?" Kaleb asked.

"Life's a gift, so you might as well enjoy it all the more when it is on the line," McBrayer replied.

"Yeah, it is an old combat trick. I've seen it used before," Kaleb said.

"Service is the duty of all men in the New Empires," McBrayer smiled.

"I know that all too well," Kaleb added.

Before McBrayer could say anything else, the door opened and another hall, this one only half the length of the lower, appeared before them running fore and aft.

"I'd guess from here we go fore," Kaleb said.

McBrayer nodded and the two of them marched quickly down the hall, closed doors with numbers on either side drifting past until they pulled up at to a reinforced metal door at the end.

"Oricalcum," McBrayer said.

"Yeah, and that means we'd better hope it isn't locked," Kaleb replied.

He tried the handle and it didn't give, a curse coming to his lips before McBrayer cleared his throat.

"You were a Dragmarsh Officer, Mr. Cross. Isn't that correct?" McBrayer asked.

"Yes," Kaleb nodded.

"Do you by chance still carry your war tag?" McBrayer asked, this time pointing to a thin opening just above another of the crystals set in the doorframe.

Kaleb reached into his shirt, felt the chain there and then pulled out his war tag, a thin pounded copper tab no bigger than a playing card. It held a series of impressions on the surface that caught the light as he held it forward.

"It looks like you know more about the Dragmarsh Navy than I'd have thought," Kaleb said.

"It is my job to know various histories," McBrayer smiled.

Pulling the war tag from his neck, Kaleb moved to the crystal and then slid the card into the slot above. After a moment the crystal glowed and then there was a distinct 'click' before Kaleb tried the door a second time.

It gave, and he removed his tag and opened it. Behind the door a large bridge sprawled out, twice the size of the *Gypsy's* and with a dozen seats and control panels filled with dials, knobs, and gauges. At the center was a command chair that provided a high view from the windows that surrounded the entire bridge.

"This isn't like any standard sailing vessel I've ever seen," Kaleb said.

"True, but if you don't mind," McBrayer said as he pointed first to himself and then to one of the seats.

"Be my guest," Kaleb replied.

McBrayer moved down into the interior and began tapping gauges at one terminal after another as Kaleb walked toward the chair at the center. The seat was made of polished leather with half a dozen conical tubes on one side and three levers on the other. He ran a finger over one lever before the sound of an explosion shook the windows of the cabin.

"What was that?" McBrayer asked.

Kaleb jumped up into the seat and stood on his toes but couldn't see anything other than the still expanding opening in the vault Brett and Stoneham had enacted minutes before.

"I'd say we have company below," Kaleb replied.

From several of the seats 'pings' sounded, and gauges long dead fluttered to life.

"We have power," McBrayer said.

"Is there anything you can do with it?" Kaleb asked.

McBrayer smiled, "Have a seat, Captain Cross, and I'll see what I can do."

Kaleb sat down and leaned into one of the conical horns and blew. Nothing happened, so he tried the next, then another, and finally the third which reverberated his exhale though the ship over a hidden speaker system.

"Skylla, it's time to get on board!"

From somewhere below another explosion sounded and then was overcome by the sound of the engines igniting. Kaleb braced himself as the ship lurched, McBrayer taking a seat and throwing a couple of levers.

The steel bridge that had connected to the ship clattered to port and the world bounced as the ship pulled off mooring pylons and breakaway tethers fell over the nose.

"We probably should have done a better job of casting off," Kaleb said.

McBrayer nodded but didn't reply, instead pushing forward on two sticks beside his seat as the opening of the hanger drew ever closer.

CHAPTER NINETEEN

SKYLLA

The Glaive shines like a lake in the morning sun, the light from it washing over me in waves of Afterglow that leach into my skin and fill me like a vessel. I thought I knew power, but until this moment I never understood what power really was. Now, however, I must try to hold it back, keep it from burning me as it did once before in the battle with Ethran...

The Humans came first, the light on their lances burning with blue radiance that lit the dark tunnel like a lantern. Skylla turned, threw out a hand and cast a rain of glowing spears down among them, screams rising up to the walkway like the chatter of birds.

Further out in the growing light of the vault's opening, she saw Stoneham and Brett running hard toward her position, but a sudden blast of heat and a ball of flame leapt from another tunnel and burst ten feet behind them. Stoneham tumbled but rose quickly, but Brett stayed slumped on the ground with his backpack aflame.

She reached out, drew in more Afterglow from the rising power of the ship and threw a wave of icy wind across the floor, the flames subsiding as Stoneham collected the dazed archeologist and pulled him back to his feet.

"Run!" she screamed.

As if in answer another fireball sailed from a far opening, this one arching toward the nose of the *Glaive*.

Hand outstretched, she flung a ball of glittering energy at the flaming sphere, the impact shattering them both in a shower of flame and light. The vault echoed with the blast, and she was thrown back into the guardrail behind her just as three arrows from below tore past. One still managed to find its mark, the head sinking into her thigh even as the magical garment she wore tried to resist it.

A curse slipped her lips and she collected another ball of power, this one shaping itself into a rocket that spat silver flames as it sped below. Three archers attempted to scramble away, but the impact of the Afterglow artillery shattered the floor and their bodies alike, part of the vault crumbling down around the corpses.

"Skylla, it's time to get on board!" Kaleb's voice rang through the hanger.

She looked down, Stoneham and Brett huffing into view on the level below.

"Hurry!" she screamed.

"It's not like I'm taking a break!" Stoneham fired back.

She raced down half the ladder, cursed when her leg flared with pain, and grabbed Brett by what remained of his backpack. She pushed Afterglow into her muscles and the power helped throw the addled archeologist onto the connecting plank like a doll. Stoneham heaved himself up faster without the added burden and the three of them raced across the bridge just as the jet engines fired.

The *Glaive* shuddered and the bridge tumbled away seconds later, the trio all breathing hard from the open entry to the lower level of the ship.

"Well, it's nice to know our lives never get boring," Stoneham wheezed.

Skylla tried to smile but her hand instead went to her thigh as she hissed.

"You'll need to get that looked at," Stoneham said before he stood and closed the portal door. From the window in the door, the ship's nose caught the light of day and turned into a blaze of golden light.

"I doubt I'll have time for that until we clear the vault and whatever lies beyond," she replied.

Stoneham nodded and helped her to her feet.

"As you say," he nodded.

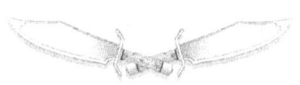

Kaleb's voice suddenly came over the speaker system again, "Battle stations!"

From the port a boom sounded and the *Glaive* shook, Skylla looking over at Stoneham who nodded.

"Brett, stay here. We've got duties," Stoneham said.

Brett nodded with a hand on his head and Stoneham followed Skylla into a long hall, Greylin at one end waving to them.

"Here's the elevator!" he called.

"Stoneham, there have to be guns on this level. Find one and see what you can do with it," Skylla said.

"Got it," Stoneham nodded, then, "Kid, you're with me. Let's find some big guns!"

Skylla moved aft, her leg half-dragging behind. Greylin passed her with a nod as she went and had to wait until the elevator 'pinged' and the doors opened. She trundled inside, ran her hand over a pulsing crystal on one wall, and then caught her breath as the car took her upward.

The door opened and she was moving again, this time to the fore and the open door to the bridge at the front of the vessel.

When she got there, Kaleb sat at a command chair, windows set around him in a hundred and eighty degree arc with McBrayer punching dials and pulling levers from a position in front of the captain.

"What is it?" she asked.

As if in answer, one of the Enlightened vessels fell into view and peppered the ship with a flare of blue fire.

"This thing is too big for this kind of combat," Kaleb grumbled.

"She probably had a nice escort of smaller vessels and picket flits when she was in service on a bombing run," McBrayer said.

Kaleb turned to her with hard eyes, and she nodded, no words spoken between them. Leaving the bridge, she made her way aft to a stair that led to an observation node at the rear of the upper deck. There, a glass bubble opened to the sky and she found a mesh tether and clip, fastened it to her belt, and then leaned into a winch until it gave. Twirling the handle round and round, she lowered her head as air burst around her, the glass bubble folding down and opening the platform to the sky.

Wind tore at her hair and water dripped from her eyes as she stood against the gale and set her boots against the metal braces on the platform. Two airships, both of Enlightened make, circled the *Glaive* like angry hornets, fire streams and wind bolts spitting out to tear at the *Glaive*'s enchanted hull. The monstrous ship shook from a fireball, and she turned to see one of the vessels coming low for a pass, three figures leaning from a shielded gondola with elemental summoned balls sparking in their hands.

She reached into the world around her, felt the Afterglow from the ship's great furnace, and pulled magic from it. The *Glaive*'s engines sputtered and the ship dipped, her knees buckling as she fell against the platform with a curse.

I can't take too much power or I'll ground her…

A fireball impacted just below the bridge, shards of glass trailing back along the hull to rip at her as they passed. She wiped blood away and tried to stand but the wound from the arrow opened again and she cried out.

A crimson stain moved down her thigh into her boot and she looked around to see the Enlightened vessel wheel away, a staccato of elemental core enhanced tracer bullets from guns on the level below chasing after it.

Nice, at least Stoneham has a gun…

Struggling to all fours, she used a rail to rise again, leaning more heavily on her uninjured leg as she recaptured the energy she'd stolen from the furnace and began shaping it. Above her a blaze of crimson energy appeared, a phoenix taking shape with wings stretching twenty feet on either side of its blazing body.

Gritting her teeth, she willed the bird forward and it dropped over the edge of the *Glaive* before rising again wreathed in crimson flame. The enemy was on the run, moving toward a billowing white cloud bank and she pointed after it, the bird beating its great wings as it sped away, the trailing vapors from its tail creating a thin line away from the ship.

Below, the guns sounded again, this time for the starboard and the second Enlightened ship came into view as the ship shook again. The enemy ship was trailing debris from multiple hits, but the *Glaive* listed suddenly and Skylla was tossed once again to the platform with a painful grunt.

Her head rang against a metal fastening and her stomach came up into her throat as the *Glaive* fell again, this time with greater force that actually lifted her off the deck and then slammed her down again when the ship leveled out.

Damn the air, give me a sea ship any day…

Looking up, the wounded enemy had turned again, but was avoiding the lower cannons as it lined up for a run across the upper level of the ship. She shook her head, manifested a ball of violet energy from the last of her stolen reserves and threw it into the air.

It held there a moment, then spread out into a fine web as the Enlightened ship drew closer, the speed of the enemy dive multiplied by the opposing speed of the oncoming *Glaive*. Pushing outward, she stretched a web of violet energy further fore, the things radius growing ever larger as the enemy ship sped on, two balls of fire coming out of its gondola to strike the armored nose of the *Glaive* with a hideous impact.

One of the fireballs ran up the nose and engulfed the bridge, smoke welling out of the shattered windows as the ship careened on toward the westerly bank of clouds.

The Enlightened ship finally saw the web, but its speed was too great to pull away and the vessel shot straight through it, the violet energy acting like titanium wire that shredded the enemy vessel, and everything in it, into a cloud of debris. Blood, bone, metal, glass, and fabric showered the upper side of the ship, and one of the elemental-based engines exploded in a firestorm of air and volcanic energies that ignited the topside of *Glaive* and scorched Skylla even as she tumbled back down the stair to avoid the oncoming apocalypse. Her safety tether caught halfway down the stair and she was jerked to a halt, her back arcing as her head struck a side rail.

Darkness swam at the edges of her vision, but a white shadow passed by and then she was lifted into a sitting position. The tether went slack and the sound of the clip release drifted in her ears alongside the ringing din of the former impact.

There was a voice but she couldn't focus on it, her eyes blinking as darkness crept closer.

The voice repeated something and she was shaken.

What will happen to Kaleb? she thought.

An image of him in jeopardy roused her and the voice became clearer, clearer, clearer until.

"Skylla!"

She jerked suddenly, her hands coming up as she focused in on the face of Vivian above her.

"What?" she managed.

"Can you walk?" Vivian asked.

Reaching down, Skylla ran her hand along the metal stair, light from a fire topside painting everything in a shifting shade of orange.

"I don't know," she replied.

"You need to try. The ship is in bad shape," Vivian said.

Skylla tried to nod, winced, and then raised a tentative hand to her forehead. It came away bloody.

"You took on hell of a hit to the head, but that is the least of our worries at the moment," Vivian said as she tried to help her stand.

Skylla leaned heavily on the woman, some of her blood having gotten into Vivian's white hair and staining it pink.

"We need to get..."

The ship lurched again, both of them spilling to the deck as an explosion ripped through the superstructure somewhere ahead.

"All hands, this is the Captain, make your way to the lower entry... now!" Kaleb's voice came across the speakers.

He's alive...

"Come on, before the elevator stops working," Vivian said.

The woman lifted her up and half-dragged her to the elevator that stood open along the hall. Once inside, she ran a hand over the crystal and the twin doors closed, Skylla sliding down a wall as the lights flickered and her stomach lurched.

"Just a bit more," Vivian whispered.

The car jerked to a halt and the doors opened, smoke filling the top of the hall outside.

"Get up!" Vivian yelled.

Skylla shook her head, but Vivian cursed her and then forced her once again to her feet.

"If you die and Kaleb lives, I'll never hear the end of it," Vivian said.

Skylla half-turned to regard the woman as she struggled to get them both down the hall. She was sweating, and up close looked slightly older than she'd remembered, but there was no mistaking a thin line of gold that whispered from her eyes like tears.

Elemental...

"You're Enlightened," Skylla managed.

Vivian didn't turn, but shook her head with a hiss of breath, saying, "That hit has you seeing things."

"No, I see it. A trace of the Enlightened blood is in you," Skylla replied.

Before Vivian could say anything else, Stoneham burst from a door with a bolt of cloth wrapped around his face.

"Stoneham!" Vivian called.

The quartermaster turned, saw the two of them, and then ran to take Skylla's weight. He shouldered under her, wrapping one of her arms behind his neck and then proceeded fore, Brett stumbling out of a hall near the middle of the *Glaive*.

"There's something out there!" Brett called.

"I know, I saw it coming up beneath us!" Stoneham shouted back. He then turned to Vivian, adding, "It's the *Gypsy*, by the banished gods, and I'm thankful to see her."

From two doors ahead Greylin stepped out, his face marked with smoke and a heavy bag over one shoulder.

"Cores!" he said, "and I found a Salvation Pack in the station as well!"

Stoneham nodded and they all moved on, Brett running in and out of view as he checked the hall and the portal door to the outside.

"Kaleb," Skylla murmured.

"He can take care of himself," Stoneham and Vivian said at the same time.

There was a pause as the two stared at one another, then they all continued on, the ship listing again as another explosion rocked the upper levels.

"Tolbert, we're leaving!" Stoneham yelled over his shoulder.

"I'm coming," the mage-tech's voice echoed up that hall.

Skylla's vision had cleared as they came to the entry, but her leg wouldn't support her and blood was still running down the side of her face. Brett's reaction to her appearance left little to her imagination, but the man took her as Stoneham passed her off and went to the outside door. With a great heave, he threw the latch and a tremendous wind sucked past them and out into the sky beyond. Vivian stumbled but caught herself against Stoneham and bits of loose debris cascaded past before the shape of the *Gypsy* rose into view.

Doc Rose was on the gondola, his hand waving as he cranked on a lever that slowly was extending a docking plank from the side of the smaller vessel. He started yelling something but they couldn't hear him, both ships engines raging and the wind at their height like a low force hurricane.

"You first!" Stoneham yelled to Vivian.

She nodded, the plank coming close enough that she could make a two foot jump to the support rail along its side. When she hit, the ships lurched again and she screamed but held on, her feet finally planting before she slowly pulled herself toward *Gypsy*.

"I'll take Skylla. You three are next," Stoneham said.

"No," Greylin protested as he took his pack off and handed it to the quartermaster, "I've got her. You go ahead."

Stoneham nodded and pushed Brett forward. Skylla leaned against Greylin and looked at him. He met her gaze and smiled.

"I owe you at least one, so don't worry. I'll fall before I let anything happen to you," he said.

A memory of their first encounter, when he'd tried to kill her, flashed through her mind but she blotted it out and nodded.

Tolbert made the leap after Brett, the mage-tech swaying with the weight of a leather tank marked 'Delta X' on his back, but both men warily found their way across the plank with Stoneham close behind.

"I guess this is it," Greylin said.

He picked her up, swung her back and then threw her forward as he jumped, the momentum helping to carry them both across before the plank swung dangerously upon impact. True to his word, Greylin held her, found the rail and then pulled himself along as the wind tore at their clothing.

She managed to look behind her, the clouds to the west flashing with orange light before the hulk of a flaming skyship burst out of the white plumes trailing black smoke and debris.

"By the banished gods," she whispered.

The Enlightened ship roared through the open air, and the *Gypsy* banked away as it grew larger and larger, but the *Glaive* was too large and wounded to evade the suicidal advance.

"Kaleb!" she screamed, but her words were lost in the wind and flame.

CHAPTER TWENTY

KALEB

Too busy to think, so watch as you can...

Fire burst over the instruments on the lead stations and Kaleb fell back, McBrayer beside him as a tortured rumble groaned though the *Glaive's* superstructure.

"We've got to get out of here!" Kaleb called over the din.

McBrayer nodded and they moved toward the exit. Running his hand over the crystal Kaleb let out a curse, the gem dead in the wall. He moved to the side, flames continuing to spread and leaned into the physical release lever, McBrayer adding his own weight until it slowly started to move. Wind howled and sucked flames into the hall beyond when the door opened, both Kaleb and his companion leaning back and shielding their faces as another explosion tore through the ship.

"She won't last much longer!" McBrayer said.

Kaleb nodded and moved toward the door, the flames having been sucked through leaving the metal frame shimmering with heat. He adjusted the glove on his hand, grabbed the side of the frame with both hands and then kicked the door open. It gave, the heated metal snapping away from the fastenings before it clattered to the deck with a great clang.

"Don't touch it. The flames have baked it good!" he yelled, but McBrayer wasn't there.

He turned around, searched the bridge and finally saw a dark circular shape in the floor. He moved through the debris and found a hatch he'd not seen from his position in the captain's chair. It was no more than three feet across and lay in a position halfway between the captain's chair and the chief pilot's station.

Damn you McBrayer...

Looking down, he saw a thin metal ladder that led to a glass observation node with a single seat. McBrayer was there, pistol in hand and an emergency parachute on his back. He looked up and provided a thin smile.

"Sorry, Mr. Cross, there was only a single chute!" he yelled up the ladder.

Kaleb shook his head but McBrayer looked away and fired his pistol, the round shattering the glass at his feet before he was sucked through into the open sky beyond.

"I'll see you in the Nine Hells," Kaleb hissed before he turned back toward the door.

Wind whipped through the portal, the metal having cooled enough to pass and the hall beyond a blackened ruin. Flames still spurted out from doors further down and shattered holes blasted in the superstructure exposed the open sky above.

He made his way forward, this ship lurching once before an impact struck with such force it lifted him up and tossed him half through one of the exposed openings. Reaching out, he caught against a beam and held on as new flames shot up from the floor.

Wind now rose up from below, the ship losing altitude as flames from the lower decks were forced up through the superstructure like volcanic geysers. Breathing hard, he climbed through the opening onto the shell of the *Glaive*, the starboard ballast pod aflame beside him and the ship trailing a huge column of smoke behind.

This is it. Saint Erik, be with me...

Setting his feet, with flames erupting around him, he dashed against the wind toward the nose of the ship. The air currents caught him half way to the tip and his feet left the plating as he leapt up and out. With hands splayed wide he sailed out into the blue, his longcoat flapping behind like a cape.

His eyes watered and he looked down, the ocean blue far below and the Island well off in the distance to the east.

Skylla...

He closed his eyes and let the wind take him, falling faster and faster until something caught his shoulders and jerked him to a sudden and violent halt.

A scream was wrenched from his lips as he opened his eyes, golden light bathing him from above as his feet dangled in the open air. He looked up to see a giant firebird flying against the backdrop of the azure sky, claws extended around his shoulders and wings flapping against the pull of gravity.

The magical bird wheeled left and up, rising slowly toward the oncoming form of the *Gypsy* as it drifted in the sterling daylight among the clouds. Kaleb smiled, the ache in his shoulders leaving him as a wave of calm washed through his body.

As he drew closer he could see figures moving in the gondola, Stoneham at the fore as they pointed, the bird coming closer until it deposited him on a plank that extended from the ships port side. Once down, the bird evaporated in a mist of gold, the tendrils flowing over him and the *Gypsy* as Stoneham moved out on the plank to help him into the safety of the gondola.

"I thought we'd lost you, Captain," Stoneham said.

"It looks like I have a guardian angel," Kaleb replied.

Vivian was there, and she touched his face, with a slight smile on hers. "You found a good one this time, Kaleb, much better than me."

He nodded and she leaned up and kissed his cheek. He stood still and she drew back, turned, but he caught her by the arm before she could walk away.

"Nice try," he said.

She looked back, the smile still there but her eyes thin and mocking.

"I never could get one past you, even when I used my womanly wiles," she replied.

"You didn't want the *Glaive*. That much seems obvious now that she's destroyed, so what was it that brought you out here?" Kaleb asked.

"It was my father's ship, Kaleb, and that means my business there is my own, but if you must push it, then just know that our bargain is done, and your precious ship is yours and yours alone."

He frowned, but let her go. She bowed slightly, first to him and then to Stoneham before moving off.

"Skylla?" Kaleb asked.

"She's with Doc Rose, and is pretty banged up, but she'll live," Stoneham replied. "She wouldn't leave the observation window until that bird was in sight with you, though."

"I figured. How did the *Gypsy* get here?" Kaleb asked.

"No idea, other than there isn't much left inside her. Practically everything that wasn't needed to hold her together must have been torn out and left in the jungle."

"What about Parish?" Kaleb asked.

"The kid will be fine, thanks to Greylin."

"Greylin?"

"Yep, he found a Salvation Pack in his gun station on the *Glaive* and was smart enough to bring it back with a half-dozen elemental cores."

Nodding, Kaleb sighed, "I knew that kid would come in handy. He's bright you know, and listens better than most, especially to stuff he probably shouldn't hear."

"Sometimes it is worth the risk to give folks a second chance to do the right thing, Captain, or so a wise man has said to me more than once," Stoneham said.

Kaleb laughed, "Well, Greylin has done so in spades."

"And what about you, Captain, you look fit as a fiddle," Stoneham said.

Kaleb looked down at his hands and then shrugged his shoulders, "I have to say I haven't felt this good since…"

He suddenly reached into his pack and something furry licked his hand.

"Lucky!" Kaleb exclaimed.

"Sir?" Stoneham asked.

"The symbiot, it must have gone into a kind of self-healing coma, but it's alive!"

Kaleb's smile was matched by Stoneham's frown, but the quartermaster shrugged, saying, "I still don't like pets."

"Well, I'll remember that before I get you a dog. Now just take me to Skylla. I think we have some unfinished business."

Skylla leaned up against the wall, a bedroll beneath her as well as a single pillow. The room was bare, otherwise, everything having been stripped and thrown out to increase lift. She had a bandage on her head, and another on her leg, but her cheeks were rosy and she carried a smile as he walked in.

"Doc wouldn't let me see you yesterday," Kaleb said.

She nodded, "I heard, and would have protested had I thought it would do any good."

"How are you?"

"Nothing a bit of magic can't heal, but I'll have to nurse it out as I can. And you?" she asked.

"I'm good, better than ever actually, thanks to you," he replied.

"I'm happy I summoned a bird instead of an artillery piece, otherwise I wouldn't have been able to catch you."

"Well, I seem to be lucky, that's for sure," he smiled.

"Speaking of lucky, I sense the symbiot, so it must still be alive," she said.

"Yes, it woke yesterday after I got back on the *Gypsy*." He reached into his pack and drew the animal out, its dark eyes staring intently at Skylla.

"The Saints watch over you and yours, Captain, as even Parish is supposed to make a full recovery," she said.

"No," he shook his head, "We all have to make our own way, and our own luck, with the people we surround ourselves with."

"Even Stoneham?" she smiled.

He laughed and shook his head, "Yeah…"

"Captain?"

Looking back at her he reached out and took her hand. "Thank you Skylla, for saving my life."

She blushed, "I think I owed you a couple."

Leaning close he gave her a kiss and then whispered in her ear, "I love you."

The air smelled of the sea, and water pooled around them as her eyes grew wide and her mouth fell open.

"Captain…" she stammered.

He put his finger on her lips and shook his head. "Just remember that."

She tried to speak but he cleared his throat and pulled his finger away, slick with seawater, before he stood.

"You get well, and I'll see to it we make it back to the *Tyger*," he said.

Nodding, he left her in the room and closed the door, his heart beating heavily in his chest.

I said it, for the first time in my life I said it and I mean it…

Moving back up the gondola to the bridge, he met Charles there, the Sky Captain turning to greet him with a smile.

"Looks like Mr. Tolbert was correct when he did his scavenging. The canister of Delta X he brought back is just as advertised," Charles said.

"Then we'll make it back?" Kaleb asked.

"Without a doubt. Our lift is just enough to clear the mountains and then make a lowland run back to Mahe."

"How long?"

"Only a couple of days if the wind holds."

Kaleb went to a window and ran his fingers along the pane. Below, the Madras stretched out almost to the horizon, but in the distance the black spine of mountains rose up to break the flat monotony of the sea.

"I wish you'd been able to recover the *Glaive*, Captain Cross."

Sighing, Kaleb kept looking out that window, "It was never about the *Glaive*, and both my wife and I knew that, as did Mr. McBrayer I would suspect."

"If it wasn't about the *Glaive*, then what was this about?"

"That, Captain Rutledge, will be answered in the future. You can bet a Findalynn brothel on that."

Captain Rutledge nodded and fell silent, the roar of the wind and the engines droning away as the *Gypsy Sky* made its way ever east toward the city and sea that was their final port of call.

GLOSSARY

Dweoller: A magical construct that has the ability to hunt creatures touched with magic. It is a kind of stick and bone bloodhound.

Drifter Guild: A loosely organized group of freebooter airship captains that keep a rag-tag fleet of flying vessels in the skies that date back to the **Final War**

Samaya: Human-like people devoid of any elemental power other than the radiant essence of their souls.

Enlightened: Highly elemental 'old races' that were locked away in the Seven Shining Cities during the Bender Invasion.

Samuel Cross: Kaleb's eldest child with Vivian Malett

Delta X: The Enlightened elemental air laced lift gas. When inert, it can be compressed into a small cylinder for long storage, but when activated it expands and can lift incredible amounts of weight for extended periods of time.

Salvation Pack: A magical healing pack used during the Enlightened Wars. One application from this enchanted kit can cure almost any bodily wound, including internal injuries.

Mage-Tech: A dying vocation of magically adept Samaya who can channel afterglow energy into constructs and engines. They helped the Samayan nations defeat the Enlightened in the Final War, but then were outcast for their use of magic once it was over. Many were killed in corrupt courts or by bounty hunters looking for a quick gold-note, and all their centers of learning were burned down as places of heresy.

Gold-Note: Bank printed notes backed by a gold standard that are accepted in the Great Five.

Great Five: The five most advanced and prestigious nations of the world that have risen from the ashes of the Final War. Also called, the 'New Empires' by many inhabitants.

Final War: The last great conflict between the Samaya and the Enlightened that ended with the Enlightened defeat that the Battle of Shaddock.

Kuhjan Empire: One of three great Empires located around the Madras Sea known as 'The Old Kingdoms'. It is roughly associated with the real world nations of India and Southeast Asia.

New Empires: The combined title of the five Great Empires of the Samaya that have risen up after the Final War.

Null Round: An anti-magic bullet designed by Samayan Mage-Techs that can break any Enlightened elemental defensive matrix.

Yanoan: The island in the Madras Sea that was home to Enlightened who had duel elements of Air and Fire giving them both long life and a desire to utilize every moment they had in creation. They were known to be master engineers in both the realms of technology and genetics.

Author Scott Taylor has worked as a writer and editor of both fantasy and science fiction for the past decade and is currently the Senior Editor for Black Gate Books, a blogger for Black Gate Magazine's Website, and the founder of Art of the Genre Publishing. He lives in Ranchos Palos Verdes, California with his wife and son where he enjoys practicing a Peter Pan lifestyle.

David R. Deitrick is a former military man turned artist who has made a career out of defining role-playing games and comics since the early 1980s. He has worked on such classics as Star Trek, Battletech, Dr Who, Traveller and Space: 1889. He currently resides in Tennessee with his lovely wife Lori.

www.ingramcontent.com/pod-product-compliance
Lightning Source LLC
Chambersburg PA
CBHW070027260626
47159CB00005B/1970